SOULS ARE FLYING!

A Celebration of Jewish Stories

SOULS ARE FLYING!
A CELEBRATION OF JEWISH STORIES

Jewish Short Stories by
Sholem Abramovitsh
Sholem Aleichem
I. L. Peretz
and
Jacob Dinezon

Collected and Retold by
Scott Hilton Davis

Published by
Jewish Storyteller Press
2016

Revised Edition

Cover design by Laurie Mugan

Drawing assistance by Sarah Evans

Illustration © iStockphoto.com/Nicholas Monu

Dinezon photograph from the Archives of the
YIVO Institute for Jewish Research, New York

Published by
Jewish Storyteller Press
Raleigh, North Carolina, U.S.A.
www.jewishstorytellerpress.com
books@jewishstorytellerpress.com

Printed in the United States

ISBN 978-0-9798156-9-0

Library of Congress Control Number: 2016902818

For My Mother

TABLE OF CONTENTS

INTRODUCTION

The stories you're about to read were written over a hundred years ago by four Jewish writers: Sholem Abramovitsh, Sholem Aleichem, I. L. Peretz, and Jacob Dinezon. Though we rarely hear their names today, these four writers were once very famous and much beloved by Jewish readers all over the world.

The reason they were so beloved was because they wrote these wonderful stories about a place we now call, "The Old Country"—the tiny towns and villages of Russia and Eastern Europe, where, for many of us who are Jewish, our *alte bobes* and *zaydes*—our great grandmothers and grandfathers—were born.

They wrote about *dos Yiddishe folk*—the common Jewish people—about their conflicts and struggles, their hopes and their dreams. How they lived their lives, how they loved, and how they tried to remain faithful to their Jewish way of life. And through their stories, these four writers have left us a cultural legacy of how to live a Jewish life, of how to hold on to our Jewish values and identity in a world that seems constantly in turmoil.

Coping with a world in turmoil was a way of life for Jews living in Russia and Eastern Europe at the turn of the twentieth century. Extreme poverty, oppressive taxation, anti-Semitism, and *pogroms*—vicious attacks by peasants and government soldiers—made daily life difficult and dangerous. Many Jews moved from rural *shtetls* to urban cities to find work and pursue modern education. Jewish stories helped people stay connected to their religious roots and traditions in a rapidly changing world.

As you read these stories, don't be surprised if they seem a little old-fashioned to you. Unlike modern literature, the stories in this book tend to wander around a bit, changing directions sometimes, and often ending with a twist or punch line. Remember, these stories were written a long time ago, and are taking you on a journey to "The Old Country." Though you won't need your passport, you will need your imagination!

Now I have to tell you something: I have a special wish for these stories. I hope you will read them aloud—like a storyteller—to your family and friends.

Why read them aloud? Well, for one thing, I wrote them to be performed in front of an audience.

But there's another reason: back when they were originally published over a century ago, Jewish families read stories aloud as a form of entertainment.

Of course, in those days, people didn't have the entertainment choices we have today. It would take decades before the invention of radio, television, computers, video games, smart phones, iPads, and internet streaming and downloads. People had to entertain themselves in other ways, and reading stories to each other became a very popular pastime, especially at night and on *Shabbes*—the Sabbath.

Sometimes, when Jews were too poor to buy books, they would rent them from traveling book peddlers who were required, like all Jews, to rest on the Sabbath. If a book peddler couldn't travel on *Shabbes,* he could at least make a little extra money loaning out his merchandise. This made books of short stories especially popular because reading time was limited, and because books had to be returned to the book peddler as soon as *Shabbes* was over.

Jewish literature became very popular during this period. In addition to religious works written in Hebrew, a large number of books and newspapers were published in Yiddish because, back then, Yiddish was the common language of the Jewish people.

Of course, we don t hear much Yiddish anymore, but it was once a rich and vibrant language—a language used to create a thriving and dynamic Jewish culture filled with poetry, plays. songs, and stories.

Unfortunately, time and tragedy have had a devastating effect on Yiddish and the people who spoke it. A great deal has been lost. but we are fortunate to have a number of stories by Sholem Abramovitsh, Sholem Aleichem, I. L. Peretz, and Jacob Dinezon available in English translations.

Which brings me to a word about my versions of these Jewish stories. Sadly, because I do not read or understand much Yiddish, I have based my versions on new or previously translated stories. I have adapted these stories to be performed, often working and reworking them like a tailor, adding a little here, snipping a little there, and moving things around until I had something that reflected what I believed was the author's original intent.

To justify my tampering with these great writers' stories, I comforted myself with a story by I. L. Peretz called, "The Reincarnation of a Melody." In this tale, Peretz relates the journey of a Jewish song through various incarnations. The melody begins life as a joyful wedding song for an orphaned bride. A small town musician hears it and plays it as a memorial song at a funeral. Next, it finds itself in a Yiddish theatre being played by a *klezmer* band. The melody becomes so popular, organ grinders play it on street corners. Then a blind girl hears it and uses it to beg for charity. A famous rabbi is so moved by it, he sings it as a *Shabbes* song. And at the end of the story, the melody is redeemed when it is again played as a wedding march for an orphaned bride.

In all its incarnations, the melody never loses its essential Jewishness, its essential goodness, or its ability to touch the heart. These are the qualities I have tried to retain in these "reincarnated stories." And these are the qualities I hope will shine through when you share these stories with your family and friends!

ABOUT THE AUTHORS

 SHOLEM ABRAMOVITSH was already a renowned Hebrew author when he turned to writing stories in Yiddish under the pseudonym Mendele Moykher Sforim, Mendele the Book Seller.

Born into a poor family in Lithuania in 1836, Abramovitsh's life became even more difficult when his father died and he was forced to join a band of wandering beggars to make a living. He finally settled in the town of Kamenets-Podolski, where he married and became a teacher.

In 1858, Abramovitsh moved to Berdichev, where he began to write in earnest, producing several satirical novels and plays in Hebrew and Yiddish. But when members of the community became offended by his writings—his satires having hit too close to home—he was forced to move his family to Zhitomir, where he continued to teach and write. In 1881, Abramovitsh became the headmaster of the Talmud-Torah, the community-supported elementary Jewish school in Odessa where he spent the rest of his life. He died in 1917 at the age of eighty-one.

In his Yiddish writings, Abramovitsh chastised the rich and powerful, and championed the poor and downtrodden. Always a teacher at heart, he wrote in Yiddish to uplift and advance the Jewish masses. Yet, he was also a consummate writer, acknowledged even in his own day for elevating Yiddish to a literary language. It was Sholem Aleichem who dubbed Abramovitsh "*the zayde,*" the grandfather, of modern Yiddish literature for being the first to create literary works of real merit in Yiddish.

*   *   *   *   *

SHOLEM ALEICHEM was the pen name of the Jewish writer, Solomon Rabinowitz, and he is probably the best known of our four Jewish writers because of a certain Broadway musical that was based on his Tevye stories: *Fiddler on the Roof.*

Sholem Aleichem was born in Russia in 1859. Before becoming a writer, he taught Hebrew and Russian, and even served for a short time as a government rabbi.

He married into a very wealthy family, and when his father-in-law died, because of Russian law, Sholem Aleichem inherited the man's fortune. With part of the money, he started a literary journal called *The Jewish Folk Library,* which he published in Yiddish.

Unfortunately, Sholem Aleichem's inheritance was lost in a Russian stock market crash, and he spent the rest of his life struggling to make a living. But Sholem Aleichem was a very prolific writer of plays, short stories, and novels, and by the turn of the twentieth century, he had become well known as a Jewish humorist—sort of a Jewish Mark Twain.

In fact, a story is told that when Sholem Aleichem first visited America in 1906, he was introduced to Mark Twain in a New York City restaurant. As the two men shook hands, Sholem Aleichem said, "Many of my readers call me the Jewish Mark Twain." And Mark Twain replied, "Many of my readers call me the American Sholem Aleichem."

With the outbreak of World War I, Sholem Aleichem and his family moved to New York City, where he died in 1916.

* * * * *

ISAAC LEYBUSH PERETZ—I. L. Peretz—was born in Poland in 1851. He was a very precocious young student in the Orthodox tradition, until one day as a teenager, he was given access to a secret library of "worldly books"—books written in German, French, and Russian about science, geography, mathematics, and world history. He had never seen books like this before, and he actually taught himself how to read them. What he learned opened his eyes to a whole new world of modern ideas.

In his early thirties Peretz became an attorney and practiced law for ten years, until suddenly—for reasons he was never able to find out—he was disbarred by the Tsarist authorities. No longer able to practice law, he moved his family to Warsaw, where he took a job with the Jewish Community Council as the chief administrator of the Cemetery Division.

Peretz's first book of Yiddish stories was published in 1890, and he would go on to write hundreds of Yiddish poems, plays, essays, and short stories, and edit several Jewish publications.

By the time he died in 1915, I. L. Peretz was Eastern Europe's leading Jewish literary figure.

*　*　*　*　*

JACOB DINEZON was born in Lithuania around the year 1852. He was orphaned while still a boy and sent to live with an uncle in the Russian town of Mogilev on the Dnieper River.

As a teenager, Dinezon was hired by a very wealthy family to tutor their young daughter. He soon became such a trusted member of the family that he was promoted to bookkeeper and, ultimately, manager of the family business.

Through this family, Dinezon was introduced to the owner of a famous Jewish publishing company in Vilna called The Widow Romm and Brothers, which published his first novel in 1877. The book, *The Dark Young Man,* became a runaway bestseller!

Moving to Warsaw in the 1890s, Dinezon quickly became a prominent figure in the city's Jewish literary circle. He befriended and mentored almost every major Jewish writer of his day, including Sholem Abramovitsh, Sholem Aleichem, and I. L. Peretz, who became Dinezon's very best friend.

But what made Dinezon different from all the other Jewish writers of his day was that he wrote from the heart and not from the head. Here's what Sholem Aleichem wrote about Jacob Dinezon:

"There is somewhere in the city of Warsaw, a tiny, spare, graying little man with tiny but spotlessly clean little hands, with a little graying beard—it once was reddish—and with kindly eyes forever smiling, even when moist with tears.

"He smokes little cigarettes rolled with his own little fingers; he drinks his own tea, made in his own little teapot; and he always sits on the same chair at the table, where he keeps hidden in an unusually well-organized fashion, other people's secrets, other people's troubles, and other people's anguish, which he holds so close to his uncommonly big heart."

During the First World War, Jacob Dinezon helped found an orphanage to care for the Jewish children made homeless by the fighting between Russia and Germany. He died in August 1919 and is buried in Warsaw's Jewish cemetery beside his friend, I. L. Peretz.

The three tales by Jacob Dinezon in this book come from the very first English translation of his autobiographical short stories, *Memories and Scenes: Shtetl, Childhood, Writers.*

ONE

MENDELE THE BOOK PEDDLER

BY SHOLEM ABRAMOVITSH

"What's your name?" That's the first question one Jew asks another, even a complete stranger, the minute they meet and rattle off a "*Sholem aleichem*," a how-do-you-do.

And when this happens, no one would even think of giving a reply: "What's it to you, brother, that you should know my name? Are we going to marry off our children to each other? I have the name I was given, and leave me alone!"

On the contrary! The question, "What's your name?" is completely natural for us Jews. It lies as easily in one's nature as it does to finger someone's new coat and ask: "How much did this cost you? How much was this fabric by the yard?"

Or to ask somebody, out of the blue, about his business, and then to outline in great detail your suggested improvements, even though he has no need for them, and can do quite well without them—as he can do quite well without you!

Asking questions for us Jews has been the order of things since the beginning of time, and to take a stand against it would amount to insanity. And so I know full well that with my initial foray into the writing of stories in Yiddish, the public's first question will be: "What do they call you, Uncle?"

My name is Mendele. Thus was I named after a great-grandfather on my mother's side, Reb Mendel the Muscovite, of blessed memory. Back in the day, he was given this name because—as the story goes—he once got all the way to Moscow trading for Russian goods. When he realized where he was, he hurried back home in the blink of an eye before they had a chance to throw him out.

But that's not the point. Oy, what foolishness!

Anyhow, just providing one's name does not end the ritual inquiry. After asking the aforementioned first question, Jews generally start up with all kinds of other questions: "Where's he from?" "Is he married?" "Does he have children?" "How does he make a living?"

Ha! More and more questions.

And this is the accepted practice wherever Jews have settled throughout the Exile. And if you want to have a decent name for yourself among our people, to show—praise God—that you are a fine person, then you must provide a proper answer.

And who am I to pick a quarrel with the world? So I am ready to answer all your questions as quickly and succinctly as I can.

My passport states my age most efficiently, although in truth, how old I am is not so easy to say. My parents—rest in peace—strongly disagreed on the reckoning of my years, but they did agree on one thing: that I was born at the lighting of the first Chanukah candle during the terrible fire that burned down the marketplace—may it never happen again.

My features, as stated in my passport, are as follows: height, middling; hair, gray; eyes, brown; nose, average; a graying beard; and under "distinguishing marks," none. That is to say, altogether nothing special. Of course, this description doesn't properly show what kind of face I have, but in point of fact, what good will it do you to know that my brow is a high one with a lot of wrinkles; that my nostrils flare out; that my face at first glance seems a bit angry; or that when I'm deep in thought, I have a near-sighted squint?

Narishkayt! Foolishness, upon my word!

Even my wife didn't interest herself in such trivialities before our marriage. She took me sight unseen on the advice of her parents and the matchmaker, and it turned out all right.

Anyhow, now you know, I'm married. And as for children, no need to discuss it. I have—no evil eye—quite a few of them.

My business, as you can see by looking at me, is holy books. In point of fact, I have attempted several livelihoods, until one day I waved my hand and said, "Feh, to the Devil with all these rackets!" And that's when I turned to the holy book trade.

Now hearing this one might believe that book peddling is the finest profession, and that I am a rich man. And on that basis, Jews—yearning after a fine livelihood for themselves—will follow each other, head over heels, one after another into the book peddling business!

Don't bother. I swear to you, Jewish children, I'm a pauper!

So, if my life is a *shlepping*, wandering, beggarly one, why the Devil did I drag myself into the holy book business?

The simple answer is: I had no choice. Since childhood I have had a certain weakness, which in the language of the *goyim* is called, "Love of Nature." That is to say, a love for everything that grows, that sprouts, that lives. Everything that's found in this world: a little blade of grass, a little rose, a little tree, a little bird. Oy, how it pulls me to it—I hope it never happens to you.

"*Vey iz mir,*" I hear you say, "how can this be? A Jew with a beard, with responsibilities, married, a father of children!"

Nu, what can I tell you? I know such things are not suitable for a Jew, but what can I do? It's my born weakness, my *yetzer hore*—my Evil Inclination—that draws me to it like a magnet.

And so the Evil Inclination—may it never happen to you, my children—said: "Mendele, book peddling is made for you.

"Pawn—even if only temporarily—your wife's bit of jewelry, buy yourself a horse and wagon, pack it up with holy books, and let yourself go forth into the world.

"If you earn, if you don't earn, it's all the same, the point is the journey—the pleasure you will receive from all the beautiful things which will reveal themselves to you in your travels.

"Your little horse will pull you along, and you will lean back, lounging like a king on your wagon. And you will look around at every tiny piece of God's beautiful handiwork: His creatures in the mountains, the valleys, the streams, the forests, and the fields.

"Then you will come into little towns and villages. There you will meet all sorts of people: fine fellows, beautiful faces, strange characters, every manner of being—crooked backs, stuck up noses, sticky-fingered, long-armed scoundrels, this kind and that kind, from the old cut and the new.

"And from your travels in the world, you will become a storyteller, and write books in Yiddish about all the places you have visited and all the Jews that you have met along the way."

And I thought to myself, "Mendele, God willing, let it be so."

Two

ETERNAL LIFE

by Sholem Aleichem

So you're wondering, Mr. Sholem Aleichem, how a citizen of Kasrilevke ended up in Paris, France? Well, I'll tell you: I got tired of going hungry every night in Kasrilevke. So I decided to seek my fortune elsewhere. As it is written, "Seek and ye shall find."

So off I went into the world, and for months I traveled from town to town trying to eke out a living, until one day I found myself on the streets of Paris—without a coin in my pocket.

The only Jew I knew in Paris was the famous banker, Rothschild. Of course, I didn't know him personally, but that never stopped me before. So I paid a little visit to Rothschild's mansion. I knocked—and the butler opened the door. He took one look at me and closed the door in my face.

I have to admit, it did not look good. But a *kasrilik* never gives up. So I knocked again, and this time when the butler opened the door, I said, "Just a minute, Monsieur Butler! I am a merchant from Kasrilevke, and I have something to sell your master that he cannot buy in Paris for any price."

Well, when this was brought to Rothschild's attention, his curiosity got the best of him, and he invited me in.

"*Sholem aleichem*—peace unto you," Rothschild said as I entered the room.

"*Aleichem sholem,* Monsieur Rothschild, and unto you peace!"

"Nu, what good news do you bring?"

"Well, Monsieur Rothschild, I have heard it said in Kasrilevke that you are pretty well off. And I don't suppose you lack for honors either. But there is one thing you do not have."

"And what is that?"

"Eternal life."

"Eternal life?"

"Yes, Monsieur Rothschild, eternal life. Life everlasting!"

His eyes grew wide. "All right," he said, "let's get down to business. Name your price."

"My price is—three hundred francs."

"Three hundred? Is that your best offer?"

"Well, I could've asked for five hundred, or a thousand, or even ten thousand. But it's too late now, I already named my price."

"Very well. Here's your money."

So right then and there, Rothschild pulls out his wallet, counts out three hundred banknotes, puts them into my hand, and I shove them into my pocket.

"All right, let's get on with it."

"Monsieur Rothschild, for eternal life, you must immediately pack all your belongings and move to Kasrilevke."

"Kasrilevke?"

"Yes, Kasrilevke. There you will never die. For as long as Kasrilevke has been in existence, no *rich man* has ever died there!"

THREE

EMPTY-HANDED

BY I. L. PERETZ

The call came up to Heaven: "Rivke-Beyle is on her death bed. Hurry Angels, get someone down here right away. Her soul belongs to us!"

"I'll go," I said. "Rivke-Beyle is a saint! This is going to be an easy one!"

So down to earth I flew, straight to Rivke-Beyle's sick-bed. *Vey iz mir,* was I in for a surprise! Standing there by the bed was a "representative" from the other place: a Dark Angel still warm from the fires of *Gehennah*—the fires of Hell!

"*Sholem aleichem,*" said the Dark Angel.

"What do you mean, *sholem aleichem?* What are you doing here?" I asked him.

"Wha'd'ya mean, 'What am I doing here?' What are *you* doing here?"

"I'm here for Rivke-Beyle's soul. She belongs to us!"

"Says who?"

"Says the Saints of Heaven, that's who! I've been sent for her soul—her pure, kind, generous soul."

"Is that so? Well, our records show that your 'pious' Rivke-Beyle had a few 'shortcomings.'"

"What are you talking about?"

"Well, for one thing, she could never get through the entire blessing over the Sabbath candles without peeking through her fingers. She could barely stumble through the words. No one could ever make heads or tails out of them!"

"We know that! But on the other hand, she never spent two seconds thinking about herself. Every minute of every day, all she cared about was feeding the hungry, healing the sick, and uplifting the widow and orphan."

"Oh, yeah?" replied the Dark Angel. "Well our records show that she would often cook and sew before the end of *Shabbes!*"

"A technicality! Sometimes kindness is impatient! This woman never failed to help a soul in need. Never refused to feed a weary body. Never refrained from lifting up a troubled heart. Look at her, Dark Angel! Rivke-Beyle never married, never took a husband, never experienced the joys of children and grandchildren. Her mind was always on one thing: helping others! Get out of here, Dark Angel. Rivke-Beyle belongs to us!"

"Huh?" gasped Rivke-Beyle. "Is someone here?"

"Now look what you've done!" said the Dark Angel. "You've awakened her!"

"Who is it?" said Rivke-Beyle in a frightened voice.

"It's me, Rivke-Beyle, an Angel of Light."

"An angel?"

"Yes. An angel sent by Heaven for your soul!"

"My soul?"

"Yes, your soul. Come with me, Rivke-Beyle?"

"Where? Where will you take me?" she asked fearfully.

"Oh, don't worry, it's all right. I've come to take you to Paradise!"

"Paradise? What's it like in Paradise?"

"Oh, it's very beautiful. With bright light shining from the Throne of Glory. White wings and a golden crown on every head!"

"A golden crown?"

"Yes!"

"And what will I do there?"

"Do there? You'll be in Heaven! You won't have to do anything there—eternal rest, everlasting happiness, radiant joy without end. Come along, I'll show you."

"But what will I do there? Is there anyone in Heaven who needs my help? A sick one to heal? A hungry one to feed? A fallen one to lift up?"

"No, not in Heaven."

"Perhaps there are lost souls there in need of rescue and comfort? You know, helping lost souls has always been my greatest pleasure!"

"No. No lost souls in Paradise. Everything is in order."

"Then what will I do there? What will I do in a place where no one needs my help? It sounds so boring!"

"Boring?"

"Excuse me," interrupted the Dark Angel.

"Who are you?" asked Rivke-Beyle.

"I am also an angel I have been listening to you, dear lady. Perhaps you will consider coming with me?"

"And where will *you* take me?"

"I will take you to the place your heart desires: a place filled with lost and accursed souls—sad and sorry souls forgotten by God."

"Oh, my heart goes out to them."

"Yes, dear lady, come along with me. You will find many in need, I promise you that. You may not be able to help them, but you will sympathize and suffer with them."

"Yes, I will go with you!"

And off they went, the saintly Rivke-Beyle and the Dark Angel. And me? I flew away—empty-handed!

FOUR

BOREKH

BY JACOB DINEZON

My name is Borekh. Just Borekh. That's what everyone calls me. Even a child, even a servant girl calls me Borekh.

And wherever I go, I am treated like a member of the family. I can sit down at anyone's table without even being asked. And whenever anyone needs something, they always call on me: "Borekh go for this, and Borekh go for that."

Who looks after me? No one, really. I have no parents or relatives. No one can even tell me where I came from. All I know is that I live here in the *yeshiva*—the study house—and that I call one of the benches, "Home."

Underneath my bench I keep a locked box which contains a clean shirt and a hat for *Shabbes*. The rest of the box is filled with knives, and sharpened nails, and pieces of wood, which I use for woodcarving.

I love to carve things for the children: animals and eagles, *dreidels* for Chanukah, and *groggers* for Purim to drown out Haman's name.

A boy once asked me: "Borekh, was your father a wood carver?"

"I don't know," I told him. "I've been an orphan for so long, I can't remember."

"Then how do you know how to carve?"

"I don't know. I just do."

But carving is nothing compared to what the Brisker can do. I have to admit the Brisker is my weak side. For the Brisker, I would do anything.

Everyone calls him the Brisker because he comes from the town of Brisk. He's the smartest boy in the whole *yeshiva*. Studying for him is like a game, and he always asks the most difficult questions.

He even argues with the Rabbi. I hardly ever understand what they're arguing about, but I always side with the Brisker!

Oh, but don't get me wrong. I have also suffered plenty from the Brisker. If he wants to play a practical joke on you, he doesn't even consider the consequences. He just does it!

And one time, he played a practical joke on me. He put something in my food that made me sick as a dog!

When he realized what he'd done, he came to me to apologize. "Borekh, I'm so sorry."

I think he was afraid that I would tell on him, and that the Rabbi would kick him out of the *yeshiva*. But I told him not to worry, and I told all the rest of the boys to keep quiet, too.

"Borekh, are you mad at me?" he asked.

"No, Brisker, I love you!"

"Love me? For what I did to you?"

"Oh no, that's over! For being so smart."

"Smart? What business is that of yours? I'm not your brother. Or even a relative."

"Oh, Brisker, what's fine is fine. Whether it's mine or not mine."

"Well, if being smart is so fine—why don't you ever study?"

"I can't study, Brisker. I can't sit still for it."

"Oh, but you can sit for hours carving those stupid little animals? Borekh, you're a fool!"

It's not that I don't try to study, it's just that other things always get in the way: a bird sits on the windowsill, a soldier sounds a bugle, a child chases after a puppy on the street. And suddenly, I've lost all track of studying.

And so, this is how I lived my life in the *yeshiva*. Going for this and going for that. And for the most part, I was satisfied. When I sighed, it was for someone else's loneliness, and when I wrung my hands, it was for someone else's troubles.

And this is how I thought my life would always be, until one day, Bunim the Matchmaker took me by the arm and said: "Borekh, tell me, how old are you?"

We were at a wedding. I was very busy "going for this and going for that." So I said, "I don't know. Who cares?" And, oh, did he get mad at me!

"It matters, Borekh! Are you already twenty? I'm asking you a very important question!"

"Leave me alone, Bunim, I don't have time for you!"

"It's time, Borekh. It's time for you to start thinking about the fact that you are not a boy anymore. Look at you, you already have a beard! It's time, Borekh, for me to find you a wife!"

I pulled away from him and ran off to serve the guests. When the band began to play, I threw myself heart and soul into the singing and dancing.

When the wedding was over, I filled my pockets with cookies and treats for my friends and headed back to the study house. But by the time I got there, everyone was sound asleep on their benches, snoring like princes.

I thought: "If I could just talk with the Brisker," but I didn't want to wake him.

So I laid down on my bench, but I couldn't sleep. I kept hearing Bunim's words ringing in my ears: "Tell me, Borekh, how old are you? You are not a boy anymore. You already have a beard!"

I touched my cheek. I could feel the hair!

"Fie on you, Bunim! A curse on you!" But then I started wondering, "How old am I? And why can't I remember?"

So I tried counting the number of *yeshivas* I've lived in. One, two, three—but I just got confused because all the *yeshivas* were the same. Same tables, same benches, same Jews praying.

The only difference was the two lions holding up the Ten Commandments over the Holy Ark. In all the other *yeshivas,* the lions were bigger, meaner, and stronger. But in this *yeshiva,* the lions look like goats! If they would let me carve a pair of lions, I would carve real lions, kings over all the other animals in the forest.

But Bunim was right about one thing: I was no longer a boy anymore, and it was time to start thinking about becoming a *mentsh.*

But how does someone become a *mentsh?*

Well, a *mentsh* is his own person. A *mentsh* makes a living. A *mentsh* lives in his own home, not in a *yeshiva.*

So how do I become a *mentsh?* If I say that I am no longer a boy anymore, who will believe me? Everyone will just laugh at me? Here, I'm just, "Borekh go for this and Borekh go for that." Master of the Universe, show me how to become a *mentsh!*

But before God could answer—

"Borekh, where are you? Bunim the Matchmaker is looking for you!"

"No, please, tell him I'm not here. Tell him he has done nothing to me, but I do not want to see him!" And then I ran. I ran from Bunim. I ran from the *yeshiva.* I ran and ran and ran.

When I returned early the next morning, everyone was asleep. I went to my bench and unlocked my box. My hand touched a little wooden animal that I had started carving but never finished. I looked at it as if for the very first time. Had I really carved this? Was this really my work?

Suddenly I forgot all about Bunim the Matchmaker. I forgot about my sadness. It was as if a stone had been lifted from my heart. Why not a woodcarver? Why not learn how to carve an entire Holy Ark with magnificent lions holding up the Ten Commandments?

But I can't do it here. Here I will always be "Borekh go for this, and Borekh go for that." I must find a place where no one knows me. A place far, far away.

Very quietly I packed all my belongings. I stood before the Holy Ark and dried my tears on the curtain.
Then I made my way to the door.

There was the Brisker, sound asleep on his bench.
How could I leave my dear friend without even saying
goodbye?

"Be a good person, Brisker. Be a great scholar. And
someday, when I hear of your greatness as a Rabbi, I will
send you a gift—something I have carved with my own
hands. A present from your old friend, Borekh—may
God protect me."

Then I kissed the *mezuzah* three times, and left the
yeshiva forever.

FIVE

THE MAGICIAN

BY I. L. PERETZ

It was one week before *Pesach*—one week before Passover—when into our little town came a Magician— a real puzzle of a man! He was ragged and tattered, and wore an old, dented top hat. He had a Jewish face with a Jewish nose, but was as clean-shaven as the *goyim*. He had no passport, and no one saw him eat—either *kosher* or *treyf*.

When asked, "Where are you from?"

He said, "Paris."

"Where are you going?"

"London!"

"How did you get here?"

"Lost my way."

If you questioned him too closely, he suddenly disappeared—poof!—as if swallowed up by the earth, only to reappear on the other side of the marketplace.

In the meantime, he rented a hall and began to perform his tricks. He swallowed burning coals, sipped a glass of water, and, "Abracadabra," pulled yards of colored ribbon from his lips—red, blue, green, yellow—as long as the Jewish Exile!

From a boot he pulled out sixteen turkeys—turkeys the size of bears! From thin air he caught gold coins—a whole pailful of them. Then he whistled and a dozen *challahs* appeared, rising up into the air like a flock of pigeons flying around in a circle above his head.

Another whistle and everything disappeared. No more turkeys, ribbons, *challahs*—everything was gone!

Though Pharaoh's Magicians may have performed greater tricks, this was more than our little town had ever seen. Still a question remained: Why is this Magician such a pauper? He pulls coins from the air, and yet he can't produce a kopeck for his rent. With a whistle he bakes more *challahs* than the biggest baker, yet his face is drawn and haggard, and hunger flares in his eyes like a flame!

A joke began to make the rounds: the Magician will be the subject of a Fifth Question at the seder this year!

But this was not the question on *my* mind one week before *Pesach*. What I wanted to know was how we were going to make Passover this year? You see, my husband, Chaim-Yone, may no evil befall him, had been out of work for nearly a year. He had once been a very successful timber merchant, but no sooner had he invested all our money in a forest, than the Tsar—a plague upon him!—decreed it a crime for Jews to cut timber! We lost everything.

So my husband took a job as a clerk for a lumber company, only to have the company go bankrupt before they could pay his wages. Then came winter—may only the enemies of Zion have such winters! We pawned everything from the chandeliers to the cushions on the chairs.

"Go to the Community Council," I pleaded. "Ask for a loan from the poor fund." But he wouldn't listen.

"Trust God, woman! God will help us. And I will not suffer the embarrassment and disgrace."

"What disgrace?" I asked him, but he said nothing. So I scoured the house, looking again in every corner, under every bed, turning everything upside down. When suddenly I found it! A spoon! An old silver spoon, lost for years! I showed it to my husband.

"God be praised!" shouted Chaim-Yone. "You, dear Feyge-Chaya, are my life!"

He grabbed my hand, and off we went to find a buyer. Finally, we would have money for *Pesach!* But the old spoon brought only a pittance, and before I could say a word, my husband was off again.

"Where are you going?" I asked.

"To the synagogue.'

"Why are you going to the synagogue?" I hurried after him and arrived just as he dropped the coins into the *tzedakah* box—the charity box.

"What are you doing?" I called out.

"Doing? I'm giving to the poor. Don't they need this money more than we do?"

"But we need money for Passover."

"For Passover, God will provide. He will not forsake us. I have no doubt."

Oy, what was I to do? I wanted to say something, but instead I remained silent. I just worried, and at night, I unburdened my heart by crying into my pillow.

My days were no better. My neighbors asked me, "When will you bake matzos? Tell us if you need something, Feyge-Chaya, and we will lend it to you." But my husband refused.

"We shall accept no gifts—except gifts that come from God."

So Passover arrived, and we didn't have enough money to buy candles. Our house was completely dark by the time my husband arrived home from the synagogue.

"*Gut yontef*, Feyge-Chaya! Happy holiday!"

"Good holiday to you, Chaim-Yone," I cried. "And a *gut yor*—a good year—to you as well."

"Why do you cry, dear wife? Today is a holiday—liberation from Egypt. Mourning is forbidden! Besides, why should you mourn at all? If the Almighty has not wanted us to have our own *Pesach* feast, we must accept His will and sit at someone else's seder table. Come, let us go and find a seder to celebrate our liberation from bondage. There is no place for tears tonight. All doors are open to us. Jews say: 'Let all who hunger come in and eat!' So come, get your shawl, and let us knock on the first Jewish door we find."

But before I could even reply, there was a knock on *our* door.

"Who's there?" asked Chaim-Yone.

"*Gut yontef!*" said a voice.

"*Gut yontef! Gut yor!*" answered Chaim-Yone.

"*Gut yor!*" replied the voice. "I wish to be a guest at your seder."

"We have no seder here. We were just on our way to find one ourselves," said Chaim-Yone as he opened the door.

"I have brought the seder with me!" said the voice.

Oy, this was too much for me, and I broke into sobs. "We're going to have a seder in the dark?"

"Of course not," replied the voice. "We have light. Abracadabra!"

Suddenly two lighted candles appeared with their flames flickering brighter than stars. The whole room glowed with light.

I looked at Chaim-Yone. He looked at me. Neither of us could believe our eyes. Standing there before us was the Magician! We stared at him in amazement.

"Table, cover yourself and come here!" ordered the Magician. Whereupon a snow-white tablecloth materialized out of thin air and fell onto the table, covering it completely.

Then the table slid across the room to the candles. Slowly the candles floated down into a pair of silver candlesticks that magically appeared on the tablecloth.

"Now, the only things missing are couches to recline on. Let there be couches!" said the Magician, and three chairs moved to the table.

"Wider!" he commanded, and the chairs widened into armchairs.

"Softer!" And suddenly the armchairs were covered in red velvet with snow-white cushions.

"Abracadabra!" he said again, and a platter of *Pesach* herbs appeared on the table, then wine glasses, and bottles of wine from *Eretz Yisroel!* Matzos appeared, and *charoset,* and everything else needed for a joyous seder, including beautiful *Haggadahs*. Before us sat a feast fit for a king!

"Is it permissible?" I asked Chaim-Yone.

"I don't know."

"You must go ask the Rabbi," I said.

"How can I leave you alone with him? *You* go ask the Rabbi."

"Me? He will think I have lost my mind!"

So we both excused ourselves and ran to ask the Rabbi.

"*Zay gezunt!*" said the Magician as we headed out the door.

We told the Rabbi everything, and he said that what is wrought by magic has no reality in this world because magic is merely an optical illusion.

"Go home," he said. "See if the cushions are soft. See if the matzos break in your hands. See if the wine fills up the glasses. If it does, all is well. This is a gift from Heaven."

So we ran back home, our hearts filled with fear and excitement. We opened the door. The Magician was gone—he had vanished completely.

But everything else was just as we had left it: the candles, the armchairs, the seder feast. We sat down on the cushions; they were soft as down pillows. We poured out the wine; it was sweet and tasty. We broke the matzos; they were thin and baked to perfection.

And suddenly we realized that this wasn't a Magician at all. It was Elijah the Prophet, who had just created for us the most holy and joyous Passover.

Gut yontef! Gut yor!

SIX

ELIJAH THE PROPHET

BY SHOLEM ALEICHEM

It's not good to be an only son. To have your parents worrying about you all the time—to be the only one left out of seven. "Don't do this. Don't do that. Wear your coat. Wash your hands!"

Ahkh, it's not good to be an only son, and a rich man's son in the bargain. My *Tate*—my father—is a money changer. He goes from shop to shop with a bag of money, changing copper for silver, and silver for copper. That is why his fingers are always black and his nails are always broken.

He works very hard. Each day when he comes home, he is exhausted. But he has a good business and people envy us for it.

Pesach has come at last—dear sweet Passover. I am dressed as befits the son of a wealthy man—like a young prince. But what good is it? I can't go out to play for fear that I might catch cold. And I cannot play with poor children for I am a rich man's son. I have such nice new clothes, and no one to show them to.

Just before sundown, *Tate* puts on his best clothes and heads to the synagogue Mama says to me: "*Tatele,* go take a little nap. Tonight you will sit at the seder table and ask the Four Questions!"

"But I'm not tired, Mama."

"I warn you: you must not fall asleep during the seder. If you do, Elijah the Prophet will come with a bag over his shoulder. He comes on the first two nights of Passover looking for children who fall asleep during the seder. He takes them away in his bag."

"Don't worry, Mama. I promise to stay awake through the entire seder."

"That's what you said last year. But you fell asleep after the first blessing."

"Why didn't Elijah come for me then?"

"You were only a small boy. Now you are a big boy. Tonight you must ask *Tate* the Four Questions. Tonight you must sing 'Slaves were we' with *Tate.* Tonight you must eat gefilte fish and matzo ball soup with us!"

"I will, Mama. Don't worry."

A little later, when *Tate* arrived home from the synagogue, he called out: "*Gut yontef!*"

And we replied, *"Gut yontef! Gut yor!"*

Then we all sat down at the seder table. *Tate* made the blessing over the wine, and I did, too. Then he drank a full cup of wine, and I did, too—right down to the last drop!

"Oy, a full cup of wine!" said Mama. " You're going to fall asleep!"

"Ha! Fall asleep? Not even if we sit here all night."

"If you fall asleep," said *Tate*, "how will you ask the Four Questions? How will you sing with me, 'Slaves were we?'"

"*Tatele*, You're going to fall asleep—fast asleep," said Mama.

"Oh, Mama, who wouldn't fall asleep if someone sat next to him singing into his ear: 'Fall asleep, fall asleep!'"

So, of course, what did I do? I fell asleep. Fast asleep. And as I slept, I dreamt that Mama got up from the table and opened the door to welcome Elijah the Prophet. And I thought to myself, "Wouldn't it be a fine thing if Elijah the Prophet came through the door with a bag on his shoulder?

And just as I was thinking this, I heard the door creak open. *Tate* stood up and cried out, "Blessed art thou who comest in the name of the Eternal."

And there he was, standing in the doorway: Elijah the Prophet. He was a handsome man—an old man with a long beard reaching to his knees. His face was yellow and wrinkled, but it was also friendly and kind. And his eyes! Oh, what eyes! Soft, joyous, loving, faithful eyes. He was bent in two and leaned on a big stick. And he had a bag on his shoulder.

Silently he came to me and said in a sweet, kind voice: "Now, little boy, get into my bag and come along."

"Where to?" I asked him.

"You will find out soon enough."

"But I don't wanna go."

"I said come along."

"How can I go with you when I'm a rich man's son?"

"Rich or poor, it makes no difference to me."

"But I'm an only child."

"Not to me!"

"My parents worry about me all the time. If they find out I'm gone, they will die—especially my mother."

"If *you* don't want to die, then come with me. Say goodbye to your mother and father and come along."

"But I am the only child left out of seven."

"For the last time, little boy, choose one or the other. Either say goodbye to your mother and father and come with me, or remain here fast asleep forever and ever."

What was I to do? I knew that going with him, God knows where, would mean the death of my mother and father. To remain here fast asleep forever and ever— would mean the death of me.

With tears in my eyes, I said: "Elijah the Prophet, dear, kind, loving Elijah, give me one more minute to think."

"Another minute," said Elijah, "but no more."

I ask you, dear reader, what would you have done? Fall asleep forever, or go with the old man and never see your parents again?

"*Tatele,* are you asleep?" asked Mama.

"Mama!" I opened my eyes. God be praised! Elijah the Prophet was gone, and Mama and *Tate* were waiting for me. It was time for the Four Questions.

And I never fell asleep at a seder again!

SEVEN

BONTSHE SHVAYG

BY I. L. PERETZ

When Bontshe Shvayg died here on earth, it left no impression whatsoever. It would have been silly to ask, "Who is Bontshe Shvayg? How did he live? How did he die? Did his heart break? Did his strength give out? Or did he simply die of starvation?

He lived like a grain of sand beside the sea: a grain of sand among millions of his own kind. And when the wind lifted him up and blew him across the sea— no one even noticed he was gone.

No family. No friends. In loneliness he lived, and in loneliness he died.

A few hours after Bontshe was buried, a terrible gust of wind knocked over his wooden grave marker. The gravedigger's wife, finding the splintered wood, used it to boil a pot of potatoes!

Bontshe Shvayg. Quiet in birth, quiet in life, and quiet in death.

But in the World to Come, Bontshe Shvayg's death was anything but quiet!

The Heavenly Shofar blared, "Teh-kee-ah!" and the angels shouted: "Bontshe Shvayg has passed away! Bontshe Shvayg is coming!"

And there at the Gates of Paradise stood Father Abraham with his arms extended. "*Sholem aleichem*, Bontshe! Welcome! I bring you greetings from God Himself!"

But Bontshe just stood there in disbelief. "This must be a terrible mistake," he thought. "They must have me confused with a rich man or a righteous rabbi."

Suddenly two angels wheeled in a golden armchair. On the chair was a golden crown glittering with precious gems. All for Bontshe Shvayg!

"What are you doing?" shouted a saint as he hurried over to stop them. "You must wait for the verdict of the Heavenly Court. Only then will we know if he stays here or goes to 'the other place.'"

"Don't be silly," said one of the angels. "This hearing is just a formality! Who would dare to say a word against Bontshe Shvayg?"

"The Prosecuting Angel for one!" replied the saint.

"The Prosecuting Angel? Nahhh!"

"How can they be so sure?" wondered Bontshe. "Oy, this must be a dream. A terrible dream! Come on, Bontshe, wake up. Wake up!" He pinched his cheeks.

"Once I dreamt that I found a pile of gold coins on the street. But when I woke up, I was even poorer than before. Once a woman smiled at me in the market-place, but when she realized her mistake, she turned away and spit. That's my fate!" He covered his eyes. "If I wake up now, I may find myself in a pit filled with snakes and lizards. *Oy vey,* if they recognize me, they may hurl me down into the burning pit of *Gehennah*—the burning pit of Hell!"

"Hear ye, hear ye. All rise for the honorable Presiding Judge of the Heavenly Court."

"Please be seated," ordered the Presiding Judge. "We are assembled here today to judge the case of Bontshe Shvayg. We shall begin with the Counsel for the Defense, the Defending Angel. Do you have an opening statement?"

"Yes, Your Honor."

"Proceed."

"His name, Bontshe Shvayg, fitted him like a glove—like a custom-made suit of clothes sewn by a master tailor."

"I object, Your Honor!"

It was the Prosecuting Angel, and his voice chilled Bontshe to the bone.

"What in the world is she talking about?" asked the Prosecuting Angel.

"Just the facts," ordered the Presiding Judge. "And be brief!"

"Yes, your Honor," said the Defending Angel. "As you know, the word '*shvayg*' in Yiddish means quiet—silent—uncomplaining. And this is how my client lived his entire life on earth. Bontshe Shvayg—Bontshe the Silent—never complained about anything—neither of God, nor of man. His eyes never flashed with a spark of hatred; his voice never raised with a claim against Heaven."

"Just the facts, Counselor!" admonished the Presiding Judge.

"Yes, your Honor. It all began at eight days with a botched circumcision—that almost ended his young life. But he did not cry out. He remained silent.

He was uncomplaining when his gentle mother died; and at the age of thirteen, an evil stepmother was forced upon him. This woman deprived him of everything: food, shelter, a Jewish education. But she was generous with her fists, and Bontshe's black and blue body showed through the holes of his torn and tattered clothes.

"He was uncomplaining when his father—in a drunken rage—seized his son by the hair and flung him out in the middle of a stormy night! Silently, Bontshe picked himself up and stumbled through the blinding snow—stumbled as far as his feet would take him—until he finally came upon a city and fell into it like a drop of water falls into the ocean.

"There, on the dangerous streets of the city, he sought the hardest work as a porter. Yet he remained silent. Bathed in sweat, doubled up under the heaviest loads, with the deepest pangs of an empty stomach, he was silent. Covered with mud, spat at, chased off the sidewalks into the street, he was silent. Staring death in the face at every moment—he was silent!

"Then one day, a change came into Bontshe's life. A fancy carriage with rubber tires flew by with runaway horses. The driver, thrown from the carriage, lay dead on the street with a fractured skull. Sparks flew from the horses' hooves; their eyes flashed like torches in the night. A passenger screamed for help. Without thinking, Bontshe leaped onto the speeding carriage and reined the frightened horses to a stop!

"The rescued man, a charitable Jew it seemed, did not forget Bontshe's good deed. He gave Bontshe the dead man's whip and made Bontshe his driver. His new Boss even found Bontshe a wife and paid for the wedding!

"But shortly after the marriage ceremony, the woman gave birth to a baby—a baby that was not Bontshe's.

The woman then deserted them, leaving Bontshe to care for the newborn child.

"What did Bontshe do? He remained silent and raised the child as his own son, giving him shelter and food from his own mouth!

"Yet Bontshe's good deed only led to heartache, for when the boy had grown strong from Bontshe's loving-kindness, he turned on his father and in a fit of anger, cruelly threw Bontshe out on the street—forcing him to wander homeless and hungry!

"Your Honor, my client was silent when the Boss went bankrupt and refused to pay Bontshe his wages. And he was silent when the Boss became wealthy again, and repaid all his debts—all, except for the money he owed to Bontshe.

"But the cruelest act of all was when the Boss, again driving in a fancy carriage with rubber tires and wild horses, ran Bontshe over in the street!

"Bontshe didn't make a sound. He didn't even tell the police who ran him over.

"He was silent in the hospital, where one is free to cry out. He was silent on his deathbed in his death agony. And he was silent when he passed away. Not a word against man. Not a word against God.

"Your Honor, I rest my case."

"Thank you, Counselor," said the Presiding Judge. "As we all know, even in such a seemingly clear cut case, it is the responsibility of the Heavenly Court to hear all the evidence and weigh both the defendant's good and bad deeds. Mr. Prosecuting Angel, you may proceed with your case."

The Prosecuting Angel stepped forward and proclaimed loudly, "Your Honor!" Then his tone softened. "Your Honor, Bontshe Shvayg was silent. I shall remain silent, too."

The angels and saints were beside themselves. For the first time in Heaven, the Prosecuting Angel was silent!

"Bontshe," said the Presiding Judge in a gentle voice, sweet as a violin. "My precious child, Bontshe. You have suffered in silence. There is not a limb or bone in your body without a wound; there is not a hidden corner of your soul which does not bleed, yet you have remained silent.

"On earth no one understood you, Bontshe Shvayg. No one could see the power hidden deep inside of you. Perhaps you yourself did not know that if you had only cried out, your cries would have broken the chains of bondage—would have shaken and shattered the mighty walls of Jericho!

"No, Bontshe Shvayg, you have never known your own strength. On earth you received no mercy for your silence. No justice. No reward. But here in the World of the Eternal Truth your reward awaits you. The Heavenly

Court will pass no judgment upon you. You, Bontshe Shvayg, may choose your own reward. You may have anything your heart desires."

For the first time, Bontshe opened his eyes. "Everything is so beautiful!" he gasped.

"Yes, Bontshe, everything here is a mere reflection of your unspoken goodness—a reflection of your soul. Everything in Heaven belongs to you. All your life you lived on nothing. What do you desire? It shall be yours."

"Anything?" asked Bontshe.

"Yes, Bontshe, anything," replied the Presiding Judge. "You will be taking only from yourself!"

"Really?"

"Yes, really."

"Then if that be so," said Bontshe in a trembling voice, "what I really want—"

"Yes, Bontshe?"

"What I really want is a hot roll with fresh butter every morning."

"Did you say, 'A hot roll with fresh butter?'" asked the Presiding Judge.

"Yes," said Bontshe, "every morning."

"Bontshe," whispered the Defending Angel, "this is your chance."

"A hot roll with fresh butter every morning," said Bontshe firmly.

A deep silence descended on the Heavenly Court. Silently the saints bowed their heads in shame. Silently the angels wept. The only sound came from the Prosecuting Angel. He just laughed!

*   *   *   *   *

Oh, how the saints and angels argued over Bontshe Shvayg's request.

The saints said this was human nature at its very best: simple and humble. Worthy of the highest praise.

The angels disagreed. "If you live your whole life on earth being silent," they argued, "letting people run all over you, not standing up for yourself or for the rights of others, then what happens when you finally get your chance before the Heavenly Court? Nothing! You're tongue tied. Silent.

"What if Bontshe had asked for an end to poverty?" the angels wondered. "What if he had asked for world peace? What if he had requested a little conversation with the Master of the Universe about His timetable for sending along the Messiah?"

They quoted Rabbi Hillel: "If I am not for myself, who will be for me? If I am only for myself, what am I? And if not now, when?"

"It takes practice to stand up for yourself," said the angels. "It takes practice to be a *mentsh*."

The debate continues to this very day.

EIGHT

MOTL FARBER, PURIMSHPIELER

BY JACOB DINEZON

Everyone used to say about the painter Motl Farber, that along with his additional soul—which we all get in honor of *Shabbes* and the holidays—he also received an additional beard.

During the week, he was a Jew with just one beard like every one else. But for *Shabbes* and the holidays, he divided his beard into two parts—half to the right and half to the left. And it looked just like two separate beards on one person! And that's what people called it: "the extra-soul beard."

"Nu, Reb Motl," people asked, "what do you do with your second beard during the week?"

"I salt it and pack it away in the same box where I pack away my stomach during the winter," Motl replied.

"When summer ends and the Master of the Universe paints the rooftops with snow, I am out of business. No longer a painter—or much of a person."

And Motl Farber was not exaggerating. When you saw him during the summer, sitting on a roof and ordering his helpers around, winter was never on his mind. During the summer he was a tall, happy Jew with broad shoulders. He sang like a cantor and his helpers responded like a chorus. Everything about his work was joyful.

But when summer was over and snow covered the rooftops, Motl Farber began to fade away. No one heard his voice, and he was rarely seen, even on *Shabbes.* Until Chanukah, Motl and his family lived on whatever profit he had made during the summer—they had *borsht* and thanked God for it. But after Chanukah, when everything was frozen, Motl lost his courage. He just lay on the bench near the stove and waited for summer.

People asked him, "How goes it, Motl?"

And he always answered with jokes: "Going? It's not going, brother, it has stopped! Frozen! Better you should ask, how does it lay? The whole winter I just lay around."

"But what are you eating in the meantime?"

"Eating? Copper pans, brass candlesticks, and for *Shabbes,* we put together a tasty little dish of pillow with feathers!"

But Motl's jokes did not comfort his wife. "Get up, do something!" she shouted. "Become a shoemaker, or a tailor, or even a water-carrier—anything but a painter, who for half a year earns a living, and then spends the other half with his teeth on a shelf. A painter is worse than a bear. At least a bear lives half the year and sleeps half the year. But a painter is awake the whole year, and wants to eat, too!"

"Yente, do you know why a bear sleeps the whole winter? Because a bear has no wife! If he had a wife, like a painter, he wouldn't be able to sleep either!"

"Oh, is that so? Just tell me, Mr. Big Shot, what would you do if you didn't have me?"

"What would I do? I'd be free as a bird! And like other birds, I'd fly off to a warmer climate and paint roofs and fences all year round!"

"Fine! Go! Fly away! Who's holding you back?"

"It's hard to fly when your wings are clipped! Oy, Yente, enough already. Another month, another week, it's closer than farther. Summer will come, and, God willing, there will be work again; our hearts will be happy and our stomachs will be full."

And every year Motl was right. The days would grow longer, little children would pour into the streets, and even the old cranky Jews who go around all winter bundled up in ten layers would begin to smile and shed a few clothes.

Motl, who had been counting the days, leaps up from his bench and recites the blessings for the month of Adar. He gives a good stretch, straightens himself up, and heads out the door. By evening he is back home with a group of painters. They shake out their pockets and collect a few kopecks. Motl's wife hurries to the marketplace and brings back bread and herring. She boils a pot of potatoes, and they all make a feast in honor of the New Moon. Then Motl divides his beard into two parts, sticks out his chest, and gives a command like a general: "Now, children, to our business! Time to organize our *purimshpiel!*"

Motl Farber's *purimshpiel*—his Purim play—is what gives Motl and his workers the money they need for Passover. Motl always plays Mordechai the Jew. Itsikl Glazer, a sturdy youth, plays Haman. Itsikl's father, Yisroel, once a soldier in Nikolai's army, plays King Akhashverus, the king of the Persian empire. And two boys—two of Motl's apprentices—play Queen Vashti and Queen Esther, a woman with a veil, a wig, and a golden crown. They even have a horse. Not a real horse, of course, but a costume Motl ties to his waist with a horse's tail on the back and a screen in front painted with big horse eyes.

For two solid weeks, Motl rehearses the actors. Then on Purim eve, right after the reading of the Megillah— the Purim story in the Scroll of Esther—everyone gathers at Motl's house. Motl ties on the horse costume, combs his beard into two parts, puts on a *shtraimel*—a fur-trimmed hat—and picks up a golden scepter. Haman—Itsikl, that is—puts on his general's uniform with a chest full of medals rented from Molotnik's pawn shop. On his head, he puts on a three-cornered military cap; and if you didn't know him, you might mistake him for a real general!

Then off they go to visit the Rabbi, who examines Vashti and Queen Esther to make certain they are really men dressed up as women. Sitting back, the Rabbi watches the *purimshpiel,* and enjoys the old custom very much! He blesses Mordechai, curses Haman, spits at Vashti, and gives Queen Esther a pat. Then he wishes the company good health and sends them on their way.

From the Rabbi, the company heads to the Community Council, where the group is served glasses of brandy which softens their hearts and raises their voices. And no matter how tight the head of the Community Council tries to be—may no shame befall him—his pleasure overcomes his stinginess, and he gives Motl a whole five rubles! With that, the company moves on, playing for all the richest people in the town.

And so the business goes from year to year: Jews are Haman's downfall, King Akhashverus orders him hanged, and everyone bows down to Mordechai the Jew who walks around with a crown on his head.

So it has always been. and so it certainly always will be. Except for the incident with the police.

The story with the police goes like this: A few weeks before Purim, a new police chief arrived in town from a distant Russian city. He had never heard of Jews, let alone any of their customs, and just before he was about to find out, Purim slipped in.

One afternoon, while leaving the police station, he came face-to-face with Motl and his whole company of Purim players. There, in front of him, was Itsikl Glazer dressed as Haman in his uniform with a chest full of medals. The police chief, thinking this was an important general, stepped back, straightened up, and brought his hand to his visor in a sharp salute.

Itsikl, trying to be polite, brought his hand up to his visor in return.

This brought a burst of laughter from the shop-keepers who were standing nearby. The police chief, realizing his error, went pale. Angrily, he ordered his men to arrest the "impostor." He then had the whole company thrown into jail.

Quickly a rumor spread: The police chief had or-dered an end to Purim Jews were beside themselves. Boys and girls, their happiness ruined, wailed in despair, "*Vey iz mir*—woe is me "

But the Eternal One always sends the cure before the plague. Earlier in the day, the police chief's wife went shopping. And out of the blue, she recognized one of the town's shopkeepers as an old friend. They greeted each other with hugs and kisses like two sisters.

What friendship, you might ask, between a Russian police chief's wife and a Jewish shopkeeper? Well, it turns out the two women had met at a summer resort in Germany many years before. While at the resort, the police chief's wife became very ill, and the shopkeeper nursed her back to health. It was only natural that the sick one felt a powerful connection to the Jewish woman.

Later, though they parted emotionally, as often happens, they gradually lost track of each other. Now, suddenly, they were reunited again. They hugged and kissed each other, and tears flowed from their eyes. The police chief's wife spent the whole afternoon at the shop and then went home with a promise to come back soon.

That evening, the Jewish woman dressed in her finest clothes and paid a little visit to the police station. It was as if the young woman had transformed herself into Queen Esther—but not so innocent and naïve—and she glowed like the morning star.

At the station, the shopkeeper was received very warmly by the police chief, who knew this was the woman who had saved his wife's life. After chatting for a few minutes—as is customary on such occasions—the pretty young "Esther" addressed the police chief:

"Your Excellency, I have a favor to ask of you."

"A favor of me? I vould do anything for you! Vhat is your request?" Of course, he said this in his own language, but it sounded like the words of the Megillah!

So the Jewish woman told him the entire story of Purim, about giving little gifts of food, and about the Purim play, the *purimshpiel*.

"Today, Your Excellency, probably because you did not know our customs, you arrested a whole company of poor, innocent Purim players. With the earnings from their performances, they were going to settle their debts from the winter, and buy provisions for the holiday of Passover."

When she finished her story, the police chief immediately ordered all the arrestees brought to him. "I vant to see your play," he said, "and you, my dear vo-man, vill translate it into Russian for me!"

Then Motl and his players were honored with glasses of cognac and commanded to perform. Merrily, the jailbirds played out the Purim story, and the police chief laughed heartily, though he didn't understand a single word.

When the performance was over, the police chief freed the *purimshpielers,* Purim was saved, and everyone rejoiced.

And from that time on throughout the town, the lovely young shopkeeper was known as "Queen Esther."

NINE

WHAT IS A SOUL?

BY I. L. PERETZ

Do you ever wonder about the soul? I think about it all the time. My friends even tease me about it. They call me "Soul Boy" because I'm always asking everyone I meet, "What is a soul?" I find it a fascinating question, don't you? But I'm getting a little ahead of myself. Perhaps I should start from the beginning.

I remember, as in a dream, when a small, thin man with a pointed beard lived in our house. Oh, how he hugged and kissed me!

Then one day, I remember the man lying in his bed. He groaned, and my mother held his hand.

One night I awoke and saw a roomful of people. "Mama," I cried, and one of the neighbors picked me up and carried me to the house next door to sleep.

When I returned home, everything had changed. There was straw on the floor. The mirror was covered with a tablecloth. And my mother sat in her stockinged feet on a small stool. When she saw me, she began to cry, "The orphan. The poor orphan."

On the windowsill, a candle was burning. Beside it stood a glass of water and a piece of cloth. Mama told me that my *Tate*—my father—had died, and that his soul had washed itself in the glass of water and dried itself on the cloth. If I did a good job of saying the *Kaddish*—the prayer for the dead—my *Tate's* soul—his *neshomeh*—would fly straght to Heaven!

And I imagined that the soul was a little bird.

* * * * *

By the time I turned fourteen, I was studying the Talmud at the home of Zorach Knip—Zorach Pinch. To this day, I don't know whether that was his real name or just a nickname because he pinched us so cruelly.

"Why do you cry?" he always laughed. "I only pinch your body! What harm will it do if the worms in the grave have a little less to eat?"

I asked him: "Reb Zorach, when the body is in the grave, what happens to the soul?"

"The soul? The soul returns to the Almighty's treasury, where it awaits another journey to this world."

And I imagined that all the souls in the Almighty's treasury were laid out like the merchandise in my mother's shop—in little colored boxes—blue, green, red, and yellow—and all tied up with fancy ribbon.

"And there in the World to Come," said Reb Zorach, "when the Almighty is ready, he lifts the soul up in his hand and blows it into a body. Whereupon an angel comes to the soul and teaches it the entire Torah—every letter, every word. But just before the soul is born, the angel gives it a quick rap underneath the nose, and the soul forgets everything it ever learned.

"For this reason, all Jewish children have a little dent above their upper lip. Go ahead, check it out for yourself. Right here under your nose."

That evening, while ice skating with my friends behind the town, I noticed that the Gentile boys, Yashek and Yantek, also had dents above their upper lips! I took my life in my own hands and said in Polish: "Yashek, you have a soul, too?"

Yashek just spit on the ground. "Vat's it to you, dog soul?"

Oy!

*   *   *   *   *

Now, at the same time I was studying the Talmud with Zorach Knip, I was also taking writing lessons from a Jewish tutor. This tutor was considered a great "freethinker" in the town—and a bit of a "revolutionary"—and the neighbors questioned his religious practices.

He was a widower, and people wondered if his daughter, Gitele—a girl about my own age—knew how to keep a *kosher* home.

But the tutor was an accomplished man, and my mother wanted her only son to know how to write a letter in Yiddish.

"I beg of you, sir, do not study any freethinking with my son," my mother demanded. "No Torah. No Talmud. No Holy Scriptures. Just teach him how to write a simple letter in Yiddish—an ordinary, 'greeting to a friend' letter."

But when I told the tutor about seeing the dent above Yashek's upper lip, he shouted at me like a madman: "*Narishkayt!* Foolishness! This is what Knip is teaching you? That only Jewish children have souls? You're a smart boy. Tell me, while you were ice skating with your friends, did you take a good look at the Gentile boys? Are their hands and feet different from yours? Do they have different eyes? Don't they laugh and cry the same way you do? Why shouldn't they have a soul the same as you?"

I couldn't believe my ears! A soul the same as me? All human beings the same? I should've run and told my mother everything. I would have, too. Except for one thing: Gitele. Sweet Gitele.

"I hope that *Tate* doesn't frighten you away," Gitele said to me one day. "Sometimes he just gets angry with the world. But he's really a very kind man. He just gets impatient. He just wants people to live together in peace—all people—Jews and Gentiles. He dreams of a better world. Is that such a bad thing?"

I didn't know what to say to her.

"*Tate* says that we Jews must be the example; that we must teach the world how to live together in peace. It's all there in the Torah, he says, if people would just follow it. Is that such a bad thing? Here, take a cookie."

Oh, Gitele.

* * * * *

When Rosh Hashanah finally arrived, I finished my year of study with Zorach Knip, and it felt like being liberated from Egyptian slavery!

I had already heard very good things about our new teacher, Reb Yoyzl. He didn't pinch, he didn't yell, he didn't even hit just for the sake of hitting.

Reb Yoyzl had been an agent for one of the great *Chassidic* rebbes. He still sold goods on commission: special oils, magic potions, even amulets. And everyone knew that Reb Yoyzl was the most reliable person in the town for charming away the evil eye!

Even before Yom Kippur, I had a chance to talk with Reb Yoyzl about the soul.

"What? Mingle with the *goyim?* Friendship with other nations! *Oy gevalt! Narishkayt!* This is what your tutor is teaching you?

"Listen to me, young man, knock those notions right out of your head! We are not like other nations. We are the 'Chosen People!'

"It is not in vain that we suffer exile, scorn, humiliation, and other plagues not even mentioned in the Torah's list of curses. If our situation were the same as the *goyim,* we would be living our lives like the *goyim!*

"Look around you. Even among us Jews, not all souls are the same. There are coarse and ordinary souls like your teacher, Zorach Knip. There are rebellious souls like your tutor, the freethinker. And there are great and righteous souls that come from beneath the Throne of Glory—souls like the most refined flour!"

And I imagined that ordinary souls were like coarsely ground flour. But the greatest souls must be filled with saffron and raisins like the special flour Mama uses to bake *challah* for *Shabbes.*

"But the main thing, young man, relates to suffering. Here in this world, the Master of the Universe, in His infinite mercy, sends us pain and suffering to remind us that we are only flesh and blood, broken vessels, insignificant. But in the World to Come, souls are washed clean through pain and suffering in the Seven Torture

Chambers of *Gehennah*—the Seven Torture Chambers of Hell."

Oy, all through the High Holy Days, all I could think about were those poor suffering souls in the Seven Torture Chambers of *Gehennah*. Then, just before Sukkos, Mama spent the whole day washing clothes. That night I dreamt that I was in the World to Come. I saw how the angels reached out their hands from Heaven and grabbed up souls that were returning from this world.

The pure souls—those white as snow—flew up from the angels' hands like doves to Paradise. But the dirty souls were thrown into a frozen sea, where dark angels soaped and scrubbed them! Then, they were thrown into a huge black pot and boiled by the fires of Hell. As the dirt was wrung out of them, and as the souls were pressed and ironed, you could hear them crying out from one end of the world to the other: "*Oy, yoy, yoy!!!*"

Then, there, among the dirty washing, I saw my tutor's soul! It had his long nose, his sunken cheeks, his pointed beard, and his thick glasses. But the more his soul was washed, the blacker it became!

"Behold the soul of your tutor, the freethinker!" shouted a Dark Angel. "Follow in his ways and your soul will become as black and *shmutzik* as his! Repent now, or your fate is sealed. Every night your soul will be washed until it is lost in the boiling pot of *Gehennah! Gehennah! Gehennah!*"

"No! No!" I cried. "I won't follow in his ways! No! No!"

"Wake up. Wake up!"

"Mama?"

"*Zunele,* what is it? You're soaking wet!"

"Mama, I was in the World to Come!"

"*Keynehore!* " she gasped and spit three times. "*Zunele,* tell me, did you see your *Tate* there?"

"No, Mama, Heaven forbid!"

"Oh, what a pity," she sighed. "He surely would have given you a message for me."

"I'm sorry, Mama."

But what good was this dream since my tutor paid no attention to dreams? For his sake, and even more for Gitele's sake, I wanted to warn him—to save him. I told him my entire dream. But the tutor just laughed and said dreams were nonsense. He wanted to show me proofs from the Holy Scriptures, but I stopped up my ears with my fingers.

It was obvious to me that he was lost, and that his punishment would be severe; that I must avoid him like the plague. That if I stayed with him, he would destroy my young soul!

But what was I to do? I promised myself a hundred times that I would run and tell my mother everything.

But I never kept my promise. Every time I opened up my mouth to speak, Gitele would appear before me like in a dream, pleading from behind my mother's back, begging me, begging me to remain silent. I felt that for Gitele's sake I was not only willing to go through fire and water, but to also be washed in the boiling pot of *Gehennah!*

And yet, I also had misgivings, because both my mother and Reb Yoyzl had very high hopes for me: that someday I would become a great Jewish scholar. So even though I was rid of my former teacher, Zorach Knip with his sharp fingernails, I was still no better off than before. And things got even worse when I turned sixteen: suddenly matchmakers started putting pressure on my mother. Matchmakers!

And me, I was still acting like a child. Every Friday night after services, I would sneak in and collect the melted candle wax from the *menorahs* in the synagogue. Then, underneath the table during class, I would mold the wax into little animals—a cat, or maybe a mouse, or even an eagle.

One day, Reb Yoyzl asked me, "What do you have in your hands?"

I was caught off guard, and I put my whole hand on the open volume of the Talmud—all five fingers with the piece of wax!

Reb Yoyzl turned pale with anger. He took a piece of string and tied my thumbs together. He picked up a ruler. "*Eints, tzfy, dry—*"

For how long? It seemed forever. But I accepted the suffering gladly; I felt that the Almighty was sending me this suffering so that I would repent and stop going to my tutor.

"Enough! You will leave the wax alone!" Reb Yoyzl commanded.

But how could I give it up? It was my greatest pleasure, creating things out of wax. And I, too, was like a piece of wax, being kneaded and molded by Reb Yoyzl, by my mother, by my tutor, and by anyone else who had the urge.

Anyone, that is—except for Gitele. Sweet Gitele. She melted me.

*   *   *   *   *

Everyone I knew considered Gitele very clever. Her father always called her, "My clever girl!"

My mother even praised her intelligence. "That Gitele is as bright as day. She'd even make a good daughter-in-law—if only she could keep a *kosher* home."

One day, while the tutor was away and Gitele was all alone, it occurred to me that I should ask her about the soul.

My knees trembled, my hands shook, and my heart pounded when I finally said, "Gitele, they say you are very smart. Tell me, please, what sort of thing is a soul?"

"A soul?" she shrugged. "I don't know."

Suddenly, she became very sad, and her eyes filled with tears.

"Gitele? What's the matter?"

"I remember that when my mother was alive, may she rest in peace, my father always said that *she* was *his* soul. They loved each other very much!"

I don't know what came over me, but at that very moment, I grabbed her hands in mine and said, "Gitele, will you be *my* soul?"

She answered very softly: "Yes."

Oh, how lucky I was in everything! Lucky that Gitele was an only daughter and I an only son, and both of us orphans, so that it was easier for us to get our own way. Lucky that the tutor had put aside a few hundred rubles for a dowry, and lucky that my mother needed the money for her shop.

I was also lucky for coming up with the idea of sending for the town *yente,* Malkeh the Matchmaker, who I promised a big bonus out of my own money if she would arrange the marriage.

But the greatest piece of luck was that I had suddenly gotten a reputation as a freethinker—and no one else would marry me!

For all that, my mother still cried over me. "If your father were to rise up from the grave and see who I am giving you to in marriage, he would return to the grave in shame."

Which gave me an idea!

"Oy, oy! Help me! Help me!"

"*Zunele, Zunele,* wake up! What is it?"

"Mama! I was in the World to Come!"

"Oy, again?"

"Yes, Mama. And you won't believe who I saw there."

"Who, *Zunele?* Who?"

"*Tate.* I saw *Tate* there!"

"*Tate?*"

"Yes, Mama. And he had a greeting for you."

"A greeting? What? What did he say?"

He said, "*Mazl tov!* "

"*Mazl tov?* "

"Yes! *Mazl tov* for making such a fine match with Gitele. He approves! He says Gitele is a very clever girl. *Mazl tov, mazl tov!* "

And that, my friends, is how I acquired a new soul.

TEN

IF I WERE ROTHSCHILD

BY SHOLEM ALEICHEM

So you see, Mr. Sholem Aleichem, I'm sitting in our little room, minding my own business, preparing a lesson for my students, when in walks my wife, long life to her.

"Nu, dear husband," she says to me, "I need money to go shopping for *Shabbes*."

You hear that, Mr. Sholem Aleichem? "Money for *Shabbes!*" Oy, how quickly the Sabbath rolls around each week. So I reach into my pocket and I pull out a few coins. She makes a face.

"You call this money?" she says to me.

"What?" I ask her. "You think I'm the banker Rothschild?"

Well I'll tell you something, Mr. Sholem Aleichem, if I were the banker Rothschild, I would make it a law

87

that every wife should carry around in her pocket a three ruble note. That way she wouldn't have to pester her husband all the time: "I need money for *Shabbes.*" She'd already have it!

And I'll tell you something else: If I were the banker Rothschild, I would buy back her old wool coat from the pawnbroker, just to keep her from complaining, "I'm always cold."

Then you know what I would do? I would go to the landlord and buy this whole house—attic to cellar—just to keep her from whining, "We need more room."

I'd say, "Here, take two whole rooms for yourself. Do whatever you want with them—cook, bake, wash, chop—only leave me in peace! All I want is *one* room so I can teach my students Hebrew. You, dear wife, can take the rest of the house, and no one will be in anybody's way."

Now, that would be the way to teach, Mr. Sholem Aleichem. Without worrying about making a living, or having money for *Shabbes,* or finding husbands for three marriageable daughters. Oy, wouldn't that be a load off my back! You hear what I'm saying? Life would be a real *mekhaye*—a real pleasure!

But let's not be selfish. What about Kasrilevke? Doesn't the town of Kasrilevke deserve a little attention, too? The synagogue needs a new roof. Wouldn't it be nice if people could pray without raindrops falling on their heads all the time?

And what about the bathhouse? I must build a new bathhouse before, God forbid, the walls come tumbling down, and we have a terrible catastrophe on our hands! And while I am at it, I will tear down the poorhouse and build a real hospital here in Kasrilevke with beds, and doctors, and medicine, and the most delicious chicken soup for all the patients.

You know, Mr. Sholem Aleichem, Kasrilevke needs a lot of things. A new home for the aged. A Society to feed the hungry and clothe the poor—so our children don't have to run around in rags all the time, showing off their *pupeks* and their *tushies.*

And what about a Loan Society, so that anyone—teacher, worker or even a merchant—can get a loan without having to pay interest or pawning the shirt off his back. And an Association for Assisting Brides, so that every poor girl old enough to stand under the *chuppah*—the wedding canopy—can be dressed and married in style.

And why only in Kasrilevke? Why not all over the world, wherever the Sons and Daughters of Zion are to be found? And because I am Rothschild, I will pay for everything, right out of my own pocket!

Of course, to bring real happiness to the world, people must be free from need. You hear what I'm saying? So I will make certain that everyone has a chance to make a living. Over a piece of bread people are ready to kill each other!

Our enemies—the Haman's of the world—what do they have against us? Do they persecute us out of plain meanness, or out of insecurity from lack of money?

I'll tell you, Mr. Sholem Aleichem, when you're not making a living, you become envious. The envy turns to hatred, and from hatred comes all the troubles of the world: all the persecutions, all the killings, and all the wars. *Wars* are ruining the world! If I were Rothschild, I would make an end to war, altogether. I would wipe it off the face of the earth.

"How?" you ask. With money, of course. I am Rothschild and I can do it!

So let's say two kings are having a little argument over a piece of land: "Territory," they call it. One king says, "This territory is mine," and the other king says, "Oh, no, it's mine. It's always been mine!"

They argue back and forth, and before you know it, armies are marching and they're shooting at each other with guns and cannons. People are dying, and blood is flowing like water.

But what if I come along and say: "Wait a minute, stop right there! What is all the arguing about? Land, boundaries, 'territory'? You only made that up. What you're really after are taxes and tariffs to fill your coffers.

But if you start a war, you will need guns and ammunition for your armies, and where will you get the money? From me, of course. You will come to Rothschild the banker for a loan.

"So stop your arguing; you don't have to fight any more. I will just give you the money!

"You, England with the checkered pants, here, take a billion. And you, Turk with the red fez, here's a billion for you. And Auntie Reysl, dear Russia, here's a billion for you, too. Use it in good health!

"And with God's help, you will all pay me back— maybe even with a little interest! Oh, not a big interest, God forbid, I don't want to get rich on you."

So you see what I've done, Mr. Sholem Aleichem? I've not only conducted a business transaction, I've stopped them from killing each other in vain. Everybody should be happy. No more wars, no more armies, no more guns, no more ammunition. No more envy, no more hatred, no more Englishmen, Frenchmen, Russians, Turks, Gypsies or Jews—not to mention them all in the same breath. The whole world will be at peace.

And as it is written, "Deliverance will come." And who knows, maybe even the Messiah.

And just think of all the money we will save!

Money! That's it! What if I abolish money altogether? I can do it, I am Rothschild!

Tell me, what is money, really? It's something we've made up. You take a piece of paper, print some pretty decorations on it, stamp it "ten rubles," and suddenly, its money.

But what is it really? *Bupkis!* Nothing! Nothing but a temptation to evil. Something everybody wants but nobody has. But if I abolish money, there's no more temptation. No more envy, no more hatred, no more evil. The whole world will be better off without money!

There's only one problem, Mr. Sholem Aleichem: Without money, what will I give my wife next week, when she says, "Nu, dear husband, I need *money* to go shopping for *Shabbes*."

ELEVEN

MAYER YEKE

BY JACOB DINEZON

I have a story for you about two men—two Jews—who unwittingly awakened in me a war that cost me many tears. A war between my head and my heart.

Both were teachers and both were poor. The first was named Mayer Yeke. He was as tall and strong as Goliath the Philistine—not to mention them both in the same breath. When Mayer Yeke prayed, his giant body swayed like a mighty tree in a fierce storm. His praying was like the roar of a lion.

Oh, how mothers prayed to have children as pious as Mayer Yeke. And we boys considered him the greatest saint. All my friends loved Mayer Yeke like life itself.

And I wanted to love him, too. But for some reason, whenever I thought about loving Mayer Yeke, my heart trembled; and every time I saw him striding down the street with his long black coat billowing out behind him, I ran away in fear.

The second Jew was named Kalman Marenhof, though only his students called him that. To everyone else in our town he was known as "Kalman the Heretic!"

Kalman was a small, handsome man, always immaculately dressed. He was the leader of the "German" *minyan*—a group that was known to be lax in their observance. They held their *Shabbes* services in the house next door to ours, and sometimes—when my father was away on business—my mother would send me there to pray. Whenever I heard Kalman sing or read Torah, his heavenly voice melted my heart.

But my friends said that Kalman was cursed. That he had sold his soul to the devil, and now his only job was to commit all kinds of sins, day and night, in order to vex God and delay the coming of the Messiah. And it wasn't only my friends who believed that Kalman was an evil man. One day, an old woman burst into the study house. She went straight to the Holy Ark, flung open the curtains, and wrapped her arms around the holy scrolls.

"Holy light-filled Torahs!" she wailed. "Where is it written that because of the sins of Kalman the Heretic, my innocent child should be taken before her time? Such a pious child, married to a brilliant scholar, and just delivered of her first child! Why must she bid farewell to this bright world and go down into a cold, dark grave? Holy Torahs, don't be silent. Fly up to God and beg Him to cancel this bitter decree. Send punishment to the guilty—to Kalman the Heretic—so we may be free from this sickness and grief!"

"Why," I wondered, "does God do things like this? Why does He let Kalman commit such sins? Why does He take His anger out on innocent babies and young mothers, punishing the innocent and not the heretic?" This grieved me so, that by the time I got home, I was so sad and depressed that I couldn't eat anything for dinner.

"What's the matter?" asked my faithful mother. She felt my head; she made me show her my tongue. When she couldn't find anything wrong, she pleaded, "*Tatele,* you must eat something." But as hard as I tried, I couldn't eat a single bite.

The next morning in *cheder,* the Rebbe told us that the preacher of Kelm was coming that afternoon to speak in the big synagogue. Those who wished to hear him could accompany the Rebbe.

By the time we got there, the synagogue was packed with people, but because the Rebbe was so well-respected by the crowd, they let us stand on a bench near the speaker's platform.

From where I stood, I could clearly see the preacher and hear his words.

"There are sins," said the preacher, "very small sins, that people don't even consider sins. Sins so small people forget to atone for them on Yom Kippur. But they are still sins, my friends

"There are other sins, sins that everyone knows are sins, and yet the person who commits them thinks they're nothing. But there, in the World Above, they are written into the Book of Life and collect into whole mountains!

"And finally, there are sins, heavy sins, sins that can destroy whole worlds! Sins so severe that the person who commits them cannot escape the tortures of *Gehennah*— the tortures of Hell! *Gehennah,* with its boiling river of pitch and sulfur; with its great pots, big as the whole world, filled with molten lead, where souls are washed clean of their evil ways!

"And do you know who this *Gehennah* is prepared for? For heretics! For Kalman the Heretic, may his name be blotted out! Repent, Kalman! Repent before it is too late!"

That night I could not sleep. I felt so angry at God for creating a *Gehennah.* I felt angry at the Rebbe for taking us, at the Kelm preacher for his words, and at Mayer Yeke. How he got into the picture I do not know, but he was always getting mixed up in my thoughts.

"Scoundrel!" I scolded myself. "How can you questions God! If God created a *Gehennah,* He knows why!"

I knew I must repent, but how? The Kelm preacher had talked about self-mortification and fasting. So I vowed to begin fasting the next morning. But then I thought, "What will your mother say? Won't she demand you eat something? How can you disobey your good and pious mother?" So I decided on self-mortification.

The Kelm preacher had said, "In summer, roll in ants, and in winter, roll in snow."

"Good," I told myself, "tomorrow I will go into the woods, find an anthill, lay on it, and let the ants crawl all over me."

But then I thought, "What if one of the ants crawls into my nose? What if it starts to tickle and I sneeze?"

So I decided to wait until winter, but then I thought, "How can I just undress in the street and roll around in the snow naked without even a shirt on? Won't people think I've gone mad? And what if I catch a cold and die? How could I ever bear it, being in the Next World when my mother is in this world, crying and mourning over me?"

So I inflicted my body in another way: I bit my arm as hard as I could until my heart clenched and tears filled my eyes. "Good!" I told myself. "God will forgive you!" But then I remembered all the tormented souls in *Gehennah*.

Suddenly, I saw Kalman there falling into a boiling pot of pitch and sulfur. I saw him struggle; I heard him scream. And there, high above him, I saw God Himself with his long, white beard, laughing in revenge at the heretic.

"What did Kalman do to make You so angry?" I asked God. But before He could answer, I thought, "What are you doing questioning God?" I bit into my arm again, but this time I didn't feel any pain. Everything was all mixed up in my head. I cried out and suddenly everything went dark.

I was very sick and lay unconscious for several days. When the fever finally passed, I felt like a depressed old man. I saw other boys playing, running, singing, joking, but I could not run after them. My heart wept, not only for myself, but also for them, for their suffering in *Gehennah*. They were unaware; they knew nothing.

Then one day, everything changed.

It was *Shabbes* and I was on my way home from the synagogue when I saw a crowd of boys shouting about something in the street. When I went to see what was going on, I saw Zalke Pinchas lying in the gutter, drunk.

The boys were throwing mud on him and yelling, "Zalke the *shiker!* Zalke the drunkard!"

I knew Reb Zalke. People said he could have been a great scholar, but in his youth he had been a student of a famous Rebbe—a genius and a saint. During one of his lessons, Reb Zalke posed a very difficult question, a question the Rebbe could not answer. The Rebbe was humiliated and cursed Reb Zalke, saying that he would never be a normal person again and that his excellent mind would never bring him any honor or respect. That's when Reb Zalke became a drunkard; and when I saw him there in the gutter, my heart melted with pity for him.

I became so angry with the boys who were making fun of him that I wanted to tear them to pieces. But there were so many of them and only one of me, so I pleaded with them to have pity on an old man. But they just laughed at me, and one of the boys yanked my ear.

What could I do? I looked around for someone to help. Suddenly I saw Kalman the Heretic coming down the street. I ran to him and begged him to help Reb Zalke. He hurried over, but when he saw what was happening, he began to laugh. "Look at that old goat wallowing around in the mud!" he said. Then he turned and walked away without a single word to the children who were still tormenting Reb Zalke.

At that very moment, I hated Kalman Marenhof with my whole heart, and wanted to yell after him, "Burn in *Gehennah,* you heretic!"

Just then, Mayer Yeke came out of the synagogue. When he heard the commotion, he came running. As soon as he saw Reb Zalke on the ground, he pulled the boys away, and I saw tears in his eyes.

"Oy, children," he said, "how can you have such mean hearts to abuse such a sick old Jew? You have no idea how great a sin this is. Go home! God will forgive you."

Suddenly, the boys regretted their actions. Mayer Yeke bent down and tried to lift up Reb Zalke. "Come, Reb Zalke, let's go home," he said gently.

But Reb Zalke pulled away from him, hit at him, and shouted, "Mayer Yeke, you're a savage! Leave me alone!"

Mayer Yeke just said, "Reb Zalke, Reb Zalke." And in his voice I heard something so deeply heartfelt, that in that moment, I saw an entirely different Mayer Yeke. In that moment, the fear that I once had for him left me completely, and I felt a joy and love for him that I had never felt for another person.

As the days passed, and as the High Holidays approached, I knew I had to apologize to Mayer Yeke. But I never had the chance. There was always a big crowd in the synagogue, and I never saw him alone on the street. Then, just before Rosh Hashanah, Mayer Yeke came to our door for a donation to help the sick and the poor.

"Son, is your mother home?" he asked.

"No, Reb Mayer," I replied. "She went out, but she'll be back soon."

My heart danced with joy. At last I could apologize to him in private. "Please come in," I said.

"Are you sure she'll be back soon?" Mayer Yeke asked.

"Yes. She is never late."

"Very well."

As he sat down at the table, the words "Forgive me!" were on the tip of my tongue, but my heart pounded and I could not get them out.

"Are you studying?" he asked.

"Yes, Torah with Rashi's commentaries," I told him.

"Very good," he smiled, and reached out to pat my head with his big hand. I quickly grabbed his hand and pleaded, "Forgive me, Reb Mayer!"

"Forgive you?" he asked in surprise. "For what?"

"Reb Mayer, I once hated you," I confessed.

"Hated me? Forgiven! Completely and absolutely forgiven. You may continue to hate me, I still forgive you everything!"

"Oh, no, Reb Mayer, I don't hate you any more. I love you. I love you as I love my whole life."

"Good!" Mayer Yeke smiled. "I have always loved you, and now I love you even more. I forgive you with my whole heart." He lifted me up in the air and gave me a big hug.

"And what about God?" I asked him.

"God?"

"Will God forgive me?"

"Of course, God forgives you. God is absolutely good. Whoever asks is forgiven."

"And what about my soul, Reb Mayer? Will it go to *Gehennah?*"

"*Gehennah?* What are you talking about?"

"The preacher from Kelm said—"

"Oy, the Kelm preacher! Do you think I understand that foolishness? How would you get to *Gehennah?* The Talmud tells us that even a non-observant Jew will be spared from *Gehennah.* Isn't it better to believe the Talmud than a Kelm preacher?"

"And what about Kalman the Heretic? Will he go to *Gehennah?* " I asked.

"Son, don't worry about Kalman," Mayer Yeke said reassuringly. "The Master of the Universe who knows the human heart sees Kalman's heart, too—how broken it is from every foolishness he commits."

"But will he have a place in the World to Come?"

"Of course! *All* Israel has a share in the World to Come. Listen, there are Jews in this world who do not earn a living and come begging for a piece of bread. Do we turn them away? No. And so we must not turn away a person who does not earn his place in the World to Come and needs others to help him out. Good and well for the one who earns his own bread, and good and well for the one who does not wait for others to perform his good deeds. Be smart, my son, and always earn your way in this world and in the World to Come."

While we were talking, my mother returned home. She gave Reb Mayer a contribution, and he thanked her for it. On his way to the door, he turned back to me and called out with such love and affection: "Remember!"

I still remember that precious "Remember" to this day. My depression lifted, and I went back to being a happy little boy again. My mother believed that Mayer Yeke had—*keynehore*—broken an evil spell, and from that day on, she always wished him long life and everything good.

TWELVE

IF NOT STILL HIGHER

BY I. L. PERETZ

Long before I ever set foot in the tiny *shtetl* town of Nemirov, I heard *bobe-mayses*—old wives' tales—about the town's legendary rabbi and his "mystical" powers. Everyone I met had an opinion about the Rebbe of Nemirov:

"Devout."

"Holy."

"Righteous as Father Abraham!"

Oy!

And talk about followers—the whole town followed the Rebbe wherever he went. When he walked, they walked. When he stopped, they stopped. When he stroked his beard, they stroked their beards—even women and children who didn't have beards!

Meshuge—crazy!

And everyone I met had a *mayse*—a story—to tell about the Rebbe. Here, let me give you a little example: a conversation I had with the town innkeeper.

"*Sholem aleichem,* stranger! Where are you from?"

"*Aleichem sholem,* Innkeeper. I come from Lithuania. From Vilna."

"Vilna! Ah, a Litvak. An intellectual, I suppose? So, tell me, Litvak, why have you come all this way to our little village of Nemirov?"

"Why shouldn't I come? I hear Nemirov is a very nice place to visit."

"So you're just passing through? Right in the middle of the High Holidays?"

"Well, to be perfectly honest with you, I do have a purpose for my visit. I have come to learn more about your famous Rebbe."

"And what do you want to know?"

"I have heard stories. I want to see with my own eyes."

"What sort of stories?"

"I have heard that every morning, during the Days of Awe—the ten days of repentance between Rosh Hashanah and Yom Kippur—the Rebbe of Nemirov—"

"Disappears. Poof! Gone! Vanishes!"

"What do you mean, 'Vanishes?'"

"What's so hard to understand, Litvak? Vanishes! You can't find him anywhere—not in *shul,* not in the *yeshiva,* and not in a *minyan.*"

"Have you checked his house?"

"Of course, we've checked his house. His house is wide open. You can go in or out just as you please."

"What about thieves?"

"Don't be a *schmendrik*! Who would rob the Rebbe? But if you were just passing by to say, "*Sholem aleichem,* hello, how are you," you wouldn't find a living soul inside. The door would be wide open, the house would be empty, and the Rebbe—disappeared! Poof! Gone! Vanishes!"

"So tell me, if the Rebbe vanishes, where does he go?"

"Where should he go? To Heaven, of course!"

"To Heaven?"

"Of course! A Rebbe has a lot to do between Rosh Hashanah and Yom Kippur! Jews—may no evil befall us—need a lot of things. Peace, health, a good livelihood, happy marriages for our children. We want to be good and holy, but sins are all around us. And Satan, with his thousand eyes, can see from one end of the world to the other. He spreads rumors and lies! And who should be of service to the citizens of Nemirov if not the Rebbe? And where can the Rebbe do the most good for the citizens of Nemirov? In Heaven, of course."

"In Heaven."

"Of course!"

"Well, Mr. Innkeeper—"

"Call me Yankele!"

"Yankele. Here's what I don't understand: How can the Rebbe go to Heaven?"

"What do you mean, 'How can the Rebbe go to Heaven?'"

"You'll forgive me. How can the Rebbe go to Heaven? As it says in the Talmud: Even Moses himself could not get into Heaven in his own lifetime!"

"Ahh, go argue with a Litvak! So, Mr. *Gantse Makher*—Mr. Big Shot—you tell me where the Rebbe goes?"

"How should I know where he goes?"

"Ehh, you Litvaks are all alike! Questions, questions, questions, but never a good answer. Feh! Who needs you?"

"Oh, I'm sure there's a good answer all right. If you think about it."

"Everything is in the *kop* with you Litvaks—in the head! Always quoting the Law. Always with an argument for everything. A heart of stone! Not like us: the *Chassidim* of Nemirov. Listen, Litvak, open up your heart to your feelings and your emotions. Sing a little. Dance a little. Maybe say a joyful little prayer. It will do you good!

"Have a good night, Litvak. And may you be inscribed and sealed for a good year in the Book of Life."

"You wish that for me?"

"Of course, Litvak, why not? I wish only the best for you. But be careful. All your curiosity about the Rebbe. All your questioning. What will it lead to?"

"Yankele, don't you want to know the truth?"

"I know the truth, Litvak. And you know it, too! As it is written: on Rosh Hashanah the Book of Life is opened, and on Yom Kippur it is closed. If you want your name inscribed for another year, then this is the time for *teshuvah, tefillah,* and *tzedakah*—for repentance, prayer, and good deeds. Not for making trouble!

"Perhaps, if you were to stay with us awhile here in Nemirov, you would come to know our Rebbe the way we know him. Perhaps then you would understand our faith, Litvak, and our ways. Sleep well!"

Sleep well. That's it! A way to find out where the Rebbe of Nemirov *really* goes when he's supposed to be in Heaven!

So that night, just before sundown, I paid a little visit to the Rebbe's house. I looked around; no one was home. I hurried into the Rebbe's room, crawled under his bed, and stretched out on the floor to wait.

Several hours passed. It became very dark. Suddenly, I heard a noise, and the Rebbe entered the room.

He sat on the bed and I held my breath. He took off his shoes, then he took off his clothes, then he pulled the blanket over him, mumbled a couple of prayers, and in less than a minute, he was sound asleep.

I, on the other hand, was wide awake, and determined to stay that way. And to keep from falling asleep, I spent the whole night reciting a complicated portion of the Talmud.

Suddenly, at dawn, there was a banging on the window shutters: "Israel, O holy folk, awake and rise to the service of the Creator!" It was the *shammes*—the caretaker of the synagogue—with the call to morning prayers. But the Rebbe was already awake. He had been tossing and turning for hours, sighing and groaning.

To hear the Rebbe of Nemirov groan is to know the sorrows of all Israel. What *tsores*—what suffering—is contained in each groan! A more fragile soul would have died at the sound of such groans. But not me. *I* am a Litvak!

Even so, I started to get a little bit nervous. This was no trifling matter, being all alone with the Rebbe of Nemirov at the dawn of such a holy day. But I refused to be frightened, and a good thing, too! Because when the Rebbe of Nemirov finally got up, I couldn't believe my eyes.

Opening an old trunk, the Rebbe began to remove clothes—not ordinary clothes, but the clothes of a Russian peasant. Linen trousers, heavy boots, a fur coat, a fur hat, and a thick leather belt studded with brass nails! Putting on the clothes, the Rebbe hurried to the kitchen where he picked up an ax from behind the stove and shoved it into his belt. Before you could say, "*Zay gezunt,*" he was out the door!

Woo hah! You think he's going to Heaven dressed like that? I don't think so! So I followed right behind him, through the darkened streets of Nemirov and out into the woods.

Stopping beside a small tree, the Rebbe lifted up the ax and began to chop. Bim, bam, boom! And the tree fell over. Chopping the tree into little logs, and the logs into little splinters, the Rebbe tied the splinters into a bundle, lifted the wood onto his shoulder, and headed back into the town.

To my amazement, the Rebbe headed down a back alley and stopped at the door of an old, broken-down shack. He knocked softly and I heard the voice of an old and frightened Jewish woman:

"Who's there?"

"Iz me." The Rebbe was talking in the voice of a Russian peasant!

"'Me?' Who?"

"Vassil. Vassil, d' voodcutter," said the Rebbe as he slowly pushed open the door of the old woman's house.

"Who are you and what do you want of me?" asked the old woman with fear in her voice.

"Firevood. I haf firevood t' sell. Very cheap!"

"Oy, who can buy firewood? Where do I, a poor widow, have money to buy anything?"

"Times are hard for you, eh?"

"Hard? Take a look around you? I'm an old woman. I haven't had heat for days. I'm freezing to death, and you tease me with firewood?"

"I'll tell you vhat: I vill leaf d' vood for you. You ken pay me for it later. Iz only six kopecks!"

"Six kopecks? Where will I get six kopecks? Why do you torment an old woman?"

"Foolish creature! I vill trust you to pay me for d' vood."

"Trust me? You don't even know me."

"I know that you are a poor, sick, Jewish voman. I know that you haf a great and mighty God. I haf faith that your great and mighty God vill provide for you. And vhen that happens, I trust that you vill pay me for d' vood. Tell me, vhere is your faith in God? Do you not trust God for a silly six kopecks virth of vood?"

"But who will light my fire? Do I have the strength to get up? And my son is working late today."

"Don't vorry. I vill light d' fire for you."

And there, in the old woman's house, I saw the Rebbe fill the stove with wood. And as he lit the fire, I could hear him, oh so quietly, recite the penitential prayers, asking God to forgive all our sins.

And when the fire was burning brightly, and the whole house was warm and cozy, I heard the Rebbe's soft, sweet voice: "For all these, O God of Mercy, forgive us, pardon us, grant us atonement."

The experience of watching the Rebbe's good deed melted my heart and changed my life forever. The Rebbe had helped the old woman without making her feel ashamed. It was a lesson in kindness and *tzedakah* that I still remember to this day.

That evening I returned to Nemirov a changed man. When Yom Kippur was over, I asked the Rebbe—long life to him—if I could become one of his students. He agreed, and as the days passed, and as I learned more and more lessons, I became one of the Rebbe's disciples— one of his best followers!

Before you know it, I settled down right here in the town, found myself a lovely wife, and started a family. Yankele the Innkeeper became my father-in-law!

And as the years flew by and as the Rebbe's legend continued to grow, people came from far and wide to hear the story: How every year between Rosh Hashanah and Yom Kippur, the Rebbe of Nemirov disappears! Poof! Gone! Vanishes!

Inevitably, someone always asks: "So where does the Rebbe go?"

And I always answer: "Where should he go? To Heaven, of course."

"To Heaven?"

"Of course!"

If not, still higher!

TRANSLATIONS

"Mendele the Book Peddler" is adapted from a new English translation by Jane Peppler from the original Yiddish novel by Sholem Abramovitsh, *Dos kleyne menshele* (*The Little Man*). New York: Hebrew Publishing Company, no date.

"Eternal Life" is adapted from a new English translation by Archie Barkan. The original Yiddish story, "*Kleyne mentshelekh mit kleyne hasoges*" ("Little People with Little Aspirations") is in *Ale verk fun Sholem Aleichem*. Vol. 6. New York: Sholem Aleichem folksfond oysgabe, 1917.

"Empty-Handed," based on the story "At the Head of the Dying Man," and "The Magician" are adapted from English translations by Henry Goodman in *Three Gifts and Other Stories by I. L. Peretz*. New York: Jewish Peoples Fraternal Order, 1947.

"Motl Farber, Purimshpieler," "Borekh," and "Mayer Yeke" are adapted from new English translations by Tina

Lunson. The original Yiddish stories are in *Zikhroynes un bilder: shtetl, kinder yorn, shraybers* (*Memories and Scenes: Shtetl, Childhood, Writers*). Originally printed by "Akhiseyfer" through the "Tsentral" society, Warsaw, no date.

"Bontshe Shvayg," "If Not Still Higher," and "What Is A Soul?" are adapted from English translations by Helena Frank in *Stories and Pictures by Issac Loeb Perez.* Philadelphia: The Jewish Publication Society of America, 1906.

"Elijah the Prophet" is adapted from an English translation by Hannah Berman in *Jewish Children.* New York: Alfred A. Knopf, Inc., 1921.

"If I Were Rothschild" is adapted from a new English translation by Jane Peppler. The original Yiddish story, "*Ven ikh bin Roytsmild,*" is in *Ale verk fun Sholem Aleichem.* Vol. 5. New York: Sholem Aleichem folksfond oysgabe, 1917.

ACKNOWLEDGMENTS

This revised version of *Souls Are Flying!* would not have been possible without the loving support, encouragement, and advice of my sister, Robin Evans, or the patience and suggestions of my niece and nephew, Sarah and Jeremy, and my brother-in-law, Jim, who sat through numerous renditions of these stories.

My love of Jewish stories was ignited in childhood by my parents, Mike and Doris Davis of blessed memory, and was nurtured by my Jewish schoolteachers, Sid and Ethel Weinstein, Sabell Bender, Morrie Molotnik, and Lenny Potash.

Years later, the flame was re-ignited by my ninth grade religious school students at Temple Beth Or in Raleigh, North Carolina. Their enthusiastic response to the stories of Sholem Aleichem and I. L. Peretz persuaded me to explore ways of adapting these works for the stage and storytelling.

Kathleen Southern offered early encouragement and story suggestions; Barbara Keys, Rabbis Lucy Dinner and Raachel Jurovics, and the Actors Comedy Lab of Raleigh provided valuable performance opportunities.

I am indebted to Cantor Mimi Haselkorn and the gracious congregants of Temple Beth David in California, and to Maxine Carr, whose Raleigh-Cary Jewish Community Center luncheon group has been a joyful and loving audience throughout the years.

Sincere thanks must also go to Aaron Rubinstein, formerly of the Yiddish Book Center, and Yeshaya Metal of YIVO for their research help, to Tina Lunson, Archie Barkan, and Jane Peppler for their wonderful new translations, to Laurie Mugan for her cover design, to Ellyn Bache for her publishing insights, and to Chris Myers and Arthur Clark for their proofreading assistance.

And finally, I am deeply grateful to Serena Ebhardt for her gentle and creative theatrical direction and to Carolyn Toben for her insight, faith, and loving support.

Scott Hilton Davis
September 2016

GLOSSARY

bobe-mayses. Grandmother stories; old wives' tales.

borsht. A cabbage or beet soup.

bupkis. Nothing; literally "goat droppings."

challah. A braided loaf of bread traditionally eaten on the Sabbath.

Chanukah. The Festival of Lights; a holiday celebrating the liberation of the Temple in Jerusalem by Judah Maccabee and his followers in the second century B.C.E.

charoset. A mixture of apples, nuts, and wine that is eaten during the Passover seder.

Chassidim. The followers of Hasidism, a mystical Jewish religious movement founded in the eighteenth century in Eastern Europe.

chuppah. The canopy under which the bride and groom stand during the wedding ceremony.

119

dreidel. A small lead or wooden top that children play with during Chanukah.

eints, tzfy, dry. One, two, three.

Eretz Yisroel. The land of Israel.

Gantse Makher. A great maker; a "big shot."

Gehennah. Hell.

Got in himmel. God in Heaven.

goyim. Non-Jews; Gentiles.

grogger. A noise-maker used during Purim.

Gut yontef, gut yor. Good holiday, good year.

Haggadah. A book or booklet containing the home Passover seder service.

Haman. The villain in the Purim story who plots to murder the Jews of ancient Persia. Esther exposes him and he is executed by King Akhashverus.

Kaddish. The mourner's prayer for the dead.

kasrilik. A cheerful pauper.

keynehore. An expression used to ward off the "evil eye."

klezmer. Jewish musicians and the style of music they play.

kop. Head.

kopeck. A Russian coin. There are one hundred kopecks in a ruble.

kosher. Food prepared according to Jewish law.

mame loshen. Yiddish; literally mother language.

matzo. Unleavened bread eaten during Passover.

mayse. A story.

Mazl tov. Good luck; congratulations.

Megillah. The scroll containing the Book of Esther which relates the Purim story.

mekhaye. Pleasure.

melamed. A teacher of young children.

menorah. A ceremonial candleholder with a central stem surrounded by six branches.

mentsh. A person; a moral and ethical person of worth and dignity.

meshuge. Crazy.

mezuzah. A small box or case that contains a small parchment scroll with two blessings from the Torah. The *mezuzah* is fastened to the doorpost of a house or building.

minyan. Ten men needed to hold a public Jewish prayer service.

narishkayt. Foolishness.

neshomeh. Soul.

Oy gevalt. Oh trouble!

Oy vey. Oh no!

Pesach. Passover; the holiday that commemorates the liberation and exodus of the Jews from Egypt.

pupek. navel; belly button.

purimshpiel. The Purim story in the Book of Esther performed as a play.

purimshpieler. A performer in a Purim play.

reb. Mister.

rebbe. A teacher; may also mean a *Chassidic* spiritual leader.

Rosh Hashanah. The Jewish New Year.

Rothschild. A Jewish family of very wealthy bankers, financiers, and philanthropists.

ruble. Russian currency. There are one hundred kopecks in a ruble.

schmendrik. A foolish person.

shmutzik. Dirty.

seder. The home Passover service and supper that recounts how God liberated the Jews from Egyptian slavery.

Shabbes. The Sabbath.

shammes. Caretaker of the synagogue.

shiker. Drunkard.

Sholem aleichem. An expression of greeting that means "peace unto you." The response to this greeting is *aleichem sholem,* "and unto you peace."

shtetl. A small Jewish town or village in Eastern Europe.

shtraimel. A fur-trimmed hat worn by a *Chassidic* rebbe.

shul. A synagogue or house of prayer.

shvayg. Quiet; silent.

Sukkos. Sukkot; the Jewish Festival of Tabernacles.

Talmud. The collection of ancient Jewish commentaries on the Torah.

tate. Father.

tatele. Little father; a term of endearment meaning "son."

tefillah. Prayer.

teshuvah. Repentance.

Torah. The Five Books of Moses; the Pentateuch; the first five books of the Bible.

treyf. Not *kosher.*

tsores. Suffering; troubles.

tushie. rear end; buttocks.

tzedakah. Good deeds; charity.

Vey iz mir. Woe is me.

Yente. A woman's name; a busybody.

yeshiva. A Jewish academy of higher learning; a study house.

Yom Kippur. The Day of Atonement.

Zay gezunt. Be well.

zunele. Small son.

ABOUT THE STORYTELLER

SCOTT HILTON DAVIS is a life-long storyteller, film-maker, author, and collector of Jewish short stories from turn of the twentieth century Eastern Europe.

Scott began his acting career as a child performing in Jewish skits and plays in Los Angeles, California. He now offers his stories and talks to synagogues, Jewish Community Centers, cultural clubs, and religious school audiences across the country.

Convinced of the historical, cultural, and ethical significance of stories by Sholem Aleichem, I. L Peretz, Sholem Abramovitsh, and Jacob Dinezon, Scott began using storytelling to bring these beloved Jewish writers' works to new audiences.

Scott is also an Emmy Award-winning public television producer. He lives in Raleigh, North Carolina.

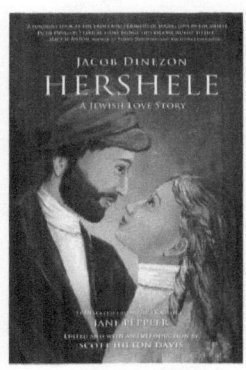